D1550259

Valley of Jewels

Valley of Jewels

MAX BRAND™

Sagebrush
Large Print Westerns

Library of Congress Cataloging-in-Publication Data

Brand, Max, 1892-1944.
    Valley of jewels / Max Brand.
        p.   cm.
    ISBN 1-57490-289-X (alk. paper)
    1. Large type books. I. Title

PS3511.A87 V27 2000
813'.52—dc21   00-040272

Cataloguing in Publication Data is available from
The British Library and the National Library of Australia.

Sagebrush Large Print Westerns are published in the United
States and Canada by Thomas T. Beeler, Publisher, PO Box 659,
Hampton Falls, New Hampshire 03844-0659. ISBN 1-57490-289-X

Published in the United Kingdom, Eire, and the Republic of
South Africa by Isis Publishing Ltd, 7 Centremead, Osney
Mead, Oxford OX2 0ES England. ISBN 0-7531-6262-8

Published in Australia and New Zealand by Bolinda Publishing
Pty Ltd, 17 Mohr Street, Tullamarine, 3043, Victoria, Australia.
ISBN 1-74030-023-8

Manufactured by Sheridan Books in Chelsea, Michigan.

Valley of Jewels

BEHIND THE DUST CLOUD

IT WAS SO HOT THAT NOBODY IN CHERRYVILLE HAD the ambition to stand up and look to see what caused the dust cloud that was rolling toward us down the road. When that dust cloud dragged closer, we could see the nodding heads of a pair of mules, in the lead team; and, pretty soon, somebody said that it must be 'Buck' Logan's mules.

That was right. It was Buck, and he brought the queerest load from the railroad that we had ever dreamed about. A load of lumber!

He pulled up at the watering trough; and he slipped the checks of his eight mules; and he let them have a drink. And while they were drinking, the steaming smell of melting pitch came rolling from the heaped and shining lumber on that big wagon and stung our nostrils.

"Buck," said someone, "who might the lucky party be that's to get that lumber?"

Buck looked up and shifted his quid; but, when the lump was settled in his other cheek, he changed his mind about answering and started checking up his mules again, pulling their heads hard to get them away from the water. Even a mule, which is too mean to be hurt by hardly anything, is a lot better off without too much cold water after a long pull.

Then Logan climbed up to his seat and called to his team; but, when they hit the collars, a mule in the swing span came back as if from a sore shoulder—and the load wasn't started.

We forgot about our question. We were all too busy calling advice and laughing at Buck and enjoying the

1

show.

Buck got into a towering rage. He was right proud of that mule team. They had cost him a good deal of money and care. He'd been here and he'd been there, getting sizes and colors that matched, and now he had a perfect set. They were all of the same gray shade to a hair. They tapered from big, sixteen-hand wheelers to mean, jack-rabbity-looking leaders, faster and smarter than you would believe. That team could pull a mountain of lead!

However, the watering trough had been overflowing; and the ground was streaked with mud, into which one of the forewheels had worked down. So Buck had a time giving his team a hitch to the left and then a hitch to the right, and trying to break that wheel out of the mud and get the wagon rolling.

It was a big load, and a couple of those mules were sore-shouldered. Even the best care in the world couldn't keep a mule or a horse from having its shoulders knocked up if they worked those rough mountain roads.

By this time nobody had any foolish idea that Buck would waste time answering questions about where that load of fine lumber was going. He was simply white with rage, to be shamed by his team in front of so many folks.

And of course we made him feel it. A hardy fellow like Buck, with a vanity about mules, couldn't be turned loose without feeling the whip. If he laid the lash on his team, we laid the lash on Buck.

We even managed to stand up to do it.

Says Rod Gruger, "It's a shame how a mule team will run downhill. That was a likely enough team about six months back. And now look at them; they can't pull a

2

paper weight off of a greased skid."

He said this sympathetic and shaking his head, and he went on, "If Buck was a fellow who would take advice, it's about time that somebody should up and tell him that a mule team like that is worth good care and good food. You can't give "em thistledown for fodder and expect them to get fat. What about it, boys?"

We agreed in a chorus, I can tell you. And Buck, he pretended not to hear; but all the time his neck kept getting redder and redder, and all the time he was getting a straighter set on his mouth. Every now and then he cursed us out of the corners of his eyes. He was a hardy-looking fellow, Buck Logan. I never seen a two-handed fighter that looked more of the part than Buck did.

But what nearly drove him mad now was the knowledge that there was nothing that human care could give to those mules that they didn't get from him. He never worked them too hard; and he was always slaving at their harness, or going out of his way to haul in supplies of crushed barley for them. And he could have made twice as much money out of them, if he had only been willing to treat them like mules and not like babies.

However, we had our good time with him.

I jumped down and got my roan horse, Jupe, and led him around in front of the big mule team. He was about as big as a minute, though he was the hardiest little jack rabbit that ever bucked off a saddle or followed a calf like a snake through a herd.

"Hey, Buck," says I, "just pass me out that extra fifth chain that you got under your wagon, and I'll pull you out with Jupe, here!"

That was more than Buck could stand. He threw

3

down his blacksnake, and he yanked the four-horse whip out of the socket and came for me.

I barely had enough time to climb into the saddle before the lash of that whip screamed past my ear. It would almost of cut my head off if it had hit me; but I got away, with a yell, old Jupe nearly jumping out of his skin to get from the path of that whip.

Buck threw his hat down in the dust and stamped on it, he was so mad; and the boys on the veranda nearly died. They simply hung onto one another and cried, they had to laugh so hard. But after a while Buck went around to his mules, and he said something at the head of each one of them and gave them a slap on the neck.

It was a wonderful thing to see him take them in hand. They had been getting more and more restless, listening to the yelling and the foolishness of that gang of cow-punchers on the porch; but Buck quieted them down, and then he went back and jumped up on the back of his near wheeler and laid his hand on the jerk line.

You could fairly see every ear in that procession of mules tip back to listen to the voice of the boss. Buck yelled, and that near leader stepped forward and took up the slack in the fifth chain, and the rest of the mules leaned just enough into the collars to get the kinks out. Then the blacksnake cut the air and cracked, and Buck yelled again.

Well, it was a pretty sight. Some people can't see anything in horseflesh except the racers with their long pedigrees and their fancy ways; but I've always seen a good deal in a work horse. They're an honest lot, you know. And work mules come right next for my admiration.

Those eight mules leaned into their collars. They

scratched like dogs until they worked their way through that surface dust and got down to a firm footing; but, when their little hoofs held, they just stiffened their legs and hung in the collars, with the hips sinking down, and the harness standing high up above their backs.

It did a man good to watch them. And that wagon lurched, staggered, and then got out of the rut—and there was the mule team breaking into a trot to keep the wagon from running over them.

We liked Buck in spite of the queer ways he had, and we couldn't help giving him a cheer when he got his heavy wagon out as slick as all that.

In the meantime, a dozen of us slid onto our horses and followed down the road to see where in the town he was going to leave that lumber.

But he didn't stop. He went right on through Cherryville and pointed the heads of those horses for the big rough mountains, where there was never a sign of a town within a good hundred miles.

A FIGHT IN THE OFFING

SOME OF US THOUGHT THAT BUCK MUST BE MAD; SOME of the rest thought that there might have been a new purchase of land in the last few weeks, and that this lumber was meant for building a new house. When we asked the sheriff—and he knew everything of importance that happened in the country—he said that there had been no sale. So where could Buck Logan have gone with that wagon?

We wished afterward that we had followed him right on. But a whole week went by before he hove through Cherryville bound in the same direction, and with

5

another load of lumber. It was dusk of the day, however; and there was nothing for Buck but to put up at the hotel.

We buzzed all around his team and his wagon while he was putting it up; and we tried everything but questions, because we knew that Buck was one of the most silent men in the world. But nothing came out of what we could see. At supper Buck sat down in the corner seat at the table—I mean, he sat in the chair that was always for me, which will be explained as I go along.

Anyway, when I came in and saw Buck seated in that chair, the boys all grinned at me, very broad and very expectant. They thought that I would tackle Buck and tell him to get out of that chair. But that wasn't my style. I've never liked fighting. And if trouble has sat down beside me more than once in my life, it hasn't been because I've invited it. I didn't like to be away from my usual place, but I thought that I could stand it for one night. So I took a chair as near the other corner as I could. By hitching my chair around to the side a good deal, I could keep my eye on the two doors that opened into the room, and there was only one window that bothered me. It opened behind my shoulder, and every minute it was like a gun pointed at my back.

However, I was willing to accept that misery even if it gave me indigestion. It was better to me than hunting for a fight with Buck Logan. And nobody could expect to get that big Logan out of a chair without a fight.

Nothing would have come out of this, if it hadn't been that the boys couldn't keep their mouths shut. They had to start talking. And about the first thing they whispered was loud enough to fetch down the table to my ears, and therefore I knew that it must have got to the ears of Logan, too.

Said some fool among the boys: "It'll happen after the supper is over. 'Doc' Willis will rip into Logan then and tear him to bits."

I could have murdered the boy who whispered that. I didn't dare to look down the table, and yet from the corner of my eye I could see Buck Logan lifting his head like a lion and glaring at me. Altogether, it was what I'd call a mean situation. I've known killings to start with a lot less. A whole lot less!

But that was not all that happened, and that was not all that was said. There was a buzz and a murmuring on all the time. Most of it was for the benefit of Buck.

I finished my meal as fast as I could and got out on the veranda and wedged myself against the wall. But still it was a long time before the little chills stopped wriggling up and down my back. I finished my first cigarette; and then a couple of the boys came out, and big Buck Logan was at their heels. He rambled straight up to me and he sings out for me and the world to hear:

"Say, kid, I understand that you're gunna eat me. Eat me raw and swaller me right down. Lemme hear what you think about it?"

He was plumb offensive, I must say; but I knew that the boys had been working Buck up to this point. He was a big man and a mean man in a silent sort of a way —which is the meanest of all—but he was not the sort of a fellow to hunt trouble. He had enough of that with his mules. So I looked him over and swallowed the first half dozen answers that jumped up to the tip of my tongue.

I merely said, "Logan, I think the boys have been talking a lot of bunk to you. I don't want any trouble with you. Not a bit! Sit down and make yourself at

7

home."

I pointed to the chair beside me and smiled at him. Nothing could have been more friendly than that, though I admit that it may have given him a pretty good excuse for thinking the thought that I saw in his face.

He simply wrinkled up with contempt and with disgust, and he turned around on his heel and strode off toward the barn.

I sat there rubbing my cheek, because I felt exactly as though I had been hit in the face. And I heard one of the lads break out:

"By the heavens, Doc is going to take it!"

And somebody else said, "Logan looks pretty big to him."

That lifted me right out of my chair, but after an instant I made myself settle down again. They could say what they pleased. The day had been—and not so very long before—when a pair of speeches like this would have made me go gunning for the biggest man in the world, with my teeth set. But I had had a good deal of the foolishness knocked out of me, and my nerves were a long distance from being what they had once been.

I had been insulted. There was no doubt of that. When a man refuses to answer a decent question and turns on his heel and walks away, it's enough insult to satisfy anybody, I suppose. But at the same time I couldn't help wanting to dodge the trouble if it were possible.

You see, Buck Logan was a square fellow, from what I'd seen and heard of him. At least, I'd seen him handle a mule team in a pinch without any brutality; and that was more than I could say about any other mule skinner I can recall. No, I felt that Buck Logan was a good fellow and that it would pay me a lot to avoid the bad

8

side of him. As for these other fellows, let them say what they wanted to about me. Words are not ounce bullets. Not by a lot they aren't!

I made me another cigarette and lighted it and snapped the match off into the darkness. I felt that I was as cool and as calm as could be, but I was wrong. I was all brittle and ready to break, and it only took a snap of the fingers to do it.

Matter of fact, I'm ashamed to tell what set me off. But a grizzly old cat that belonged in the hotel came sauntering down the porch, and I wanted to show how easy and careless I was by pretending not to notice the eyes that were on me and the smiles and the wonder and the contempt that was showing on their faces. But when I reached out my hand and talked soft to the cat, it arched its back and spat at me, and then it jumped off the veranda into the night.

That brought a roar of laughter. I don't know why. But it sent a rush of red-hot blood spinning into my brain. I jumped up from my chair and walked over where the rest of the boys were.

"Are you laughing at me?" said I.

That sobered them. But even when they were silent, I was still raging.

"I asked you if you was laughing at me, by any chance. Do I hear you answer?"

Then somebody lost in the shadows in the rear drawled: "You better ask Buck Logan about that."

I yelled, "Curse Buck Logan! Some of you go tell him that I say he's a rat; and that if he don't come here to me I'll come to find him; and there ain't any hole deep enough to hide him from me."

Then I began to walk up and down that veranda, hotter than ever. But I wasn't so angry that I didn't

9

notice two or three of the boys detach themselves and wander off toward the barn. So I knew that Logan would hear what I had said, and hear it with trimmings, too. And I knew that that was apt to make for a gun-fight—the very thing that I had dodged safely for two whole years, and that I had vowed I would never go through with again. However, a man can't change his nature. I was raised too much around guns. And I had spent too many years in Mexico—a wild and bad place, believe me.

After a little time I heard footsteps coming, and in the lead there was a long, heavy stride that I figured must be Buck Logan. Yes, here he came, right up the steps out of the night, and stood there under the gasoline lamp.

I said to myself that he was as good as a dead man, that minute. I was full of concentrated poison, and full of concentrated coldness, too. What happens in moments like that are a blur to some people; a blur to most honest men. I suppose—but not to me. When the devil takes me by the throat he multiplies me by ten, and I felt the strength of ten in me at that moment.

I saw Buck Logan as complete as though he were painted by my hand in oils. I saw his faded blue shirt, and the wrinkles in his overalls around the knees, and the hard knot of his bandanna around his neck, and the sun-stained felt hat on his head. I saw the low, handy fit of the Colt at his right hip, too; and I looked through his pale-blue eyes into his soul and thought that he was as brave and as stern a man as I had ever seen in my life—but that made no difference. I was set for a kill, and I looked on Logan as a man living but already more than half dead.

He looked me over, too. He was just as calm as me, but there was no fire in his eyes. His hands were his best

10

weapons, and not his guns; I could tell that, I thought.

Then he said, "Willis, I hear that you've been saying hard things about me."

"I'll say them over again, if you want to hear them," said I.

"I don't want to hear them," said Logan. "If I do hear them, I'll have to fight you. And I'm not ready to start pushing the daisies."

A TRY-OUT

WELL, TAKE THE TIME AND THE PLACE AND THE REST into consideration, and you'll have to admit that that was a good deal of a speech for a man to make. But though those boys who stood around and watched were a hardy gang as ever stepped, not one of them smiled and not one of them made the mistake of thinking that Buck was taking water.

I didn't make that mistake, either. I sat down again in my chair.

I said, "Buck, the trouble was that you made a mite of a mistake about me; but I never made any mistake about you. I don't want any trouble with you if I can avoid it. I feel plumb friendly to you, if you'll give me a chance to act that way."

"Friend," says Buck Logan, "is a word that I don't use more than once every ten years; but maybe I could make an exception this evening. We'll shake hands, if you say the word."

Yes, we did shake hands, and when those big bony fingers of his closed over mine they made me feel as weak as a baby. He sat down and turned his big head toward the others.

"Scatter, kids," said he. "This here is a time for man talk, and you're too young to listen."

They didn't wait to be invited twice. They just faded away here and there, and we were left alone.

"It was the little roan hoss," said Buck, after a time.

I nodded.

"Here's the makings," said I; "smoke up."

He shook his head and pulled out a black pipe. Then he whittled some shavings off of a black plug, and filled his bowl with that stuff; and when he lighted up, a cloud of smoke that would of killed mosquitoes filled the air. There was no doubt about Buck being a man-sized man. One whiff of that pipe smoke of his was enough to settle the question. It made me fair dizzy.

"It was the roan," said Buck again.

"Sure," said I, and nodded again. "I understand."

About ten minutes later he added, "My mules is close to me, Willis."

"Sure," said I. "I understand."

And, about half an hour later he said, "Time for me to turn in. This here was a fine talk, Willis."

And he went off to bed.

You can count the words that had gone to the making of that 'fine talk'. But I felt that I knew Buck, and he felt that he knew me.

I turned out at the first crack of day, because I've ridden the range so long that the sun doesn't let me sleep late; and, when I came down, there were the mules all strung out in front of the load of lumber, and Buck hitching them in their places. He must have got up an hour before the light began, because he had that whole team fed and harnessed and curried down as slick as a whistle.

I stepped out and gave him a hand till he warned me

12

to stop.

"They know their boss," said Buck Logan; "but with strangers, they think that they're tigers and that they can live on raw meat. Mind the heels of that gray devil on the off point."

I side-stepped just as the heels of the off-pointer whistled past my ear.

Buck Logan stepped back to his place and took hold on the jerk line.

"Look here, Doc," said he, "what's your job?"

"I still got most of a month's wages to blow in," said I.

"How come?"

"Poker has been good to me."

"Poker," says he, and grins; "and then what?"

"I got the best cutting hoss on the range," said I. "I'll pick me up a job, when that money is blowed in!"

"Fine," says he. "Riding range?"

"Riding herd, I suppose."

"How about man-sized work, Doc?"

"I dunno what you mean."

"Real pay."

"What kind?"

"Fifty a week."

I whistled. "That's better than ten," said I.

"Does it sound to you?"

"Not a bit."

"Why not? Like poker better?"

"No, poker always licks me in the end."

"Well?"

"I'm not a fifty-dollar-a-week man, Buck. Fifty a month is more to my style."

"No chances, eh?"

"Buck," said I, "how old am I?"

13

"Thirty-two," says he, quick as a wink.

"You miss me by seven years," I told him.

"You're not thirty-nine," said he.

"I'm not."

"The devil!" said Buck. "Are you only a kid of twenty-five?"

"I'm twenty-five," said I; "but I'm not a kid."

"You wear your gray hair right along with me," said he. "And you ain't got the fool look."

"I've had the foolishness shot out of me," said I.

He nodded. "I had a pal fifteen years ago that was that way. Quietest man that ever lived; but he was like you, one of these here lion tamers."

"Go easy, partner," said I.

"I'm not kidding you," said Buck Logan. "If you've been shot up so much that seven years have leaked out with the blood—why, I'm not fool enough to talk down to you. Only this job I'd—"

"I ain't tempted," said I.

"Why not?"

"I hate fighting."

"I didn't say that."

"No, but I guess that. Fifty a week in these days means one of two things—crooked work or guns. Well, you're not a crook, Buck."

"Thanks," said he. "But fifty a week is fifty a week."

"It depends on how long the weeks last."

"I know, but this job is different. It ain't dangerous, but it may be. You better saddle your hoss and come along."

"I have swore off on being a fool," said I.

"Swear on again," said Buck; "you're too young to miss the fun."

"Buck," said I, "it's fine of you; but it won't do. I'd

14

like to be with you, but I won't go."

He only grinned. "I've planted the poison in you," said Buck. "I'm taking the Creek road, and I'll expect you to catch up with me by noon. So long till then, kid."

He hollered to his mules. They hit their collars with a snap, and the big wagon with its shining load of white lumber rolled on down the road.

I turned my back on it after I had watched it out of sight, but when I walked back to the hotel I heard a rumbling of distant thunder and turned around with a start. I could see nothing, but I knew that that was the big wagon crossing the bridge and turning onto the Creek road.

Who the devil would want to cart good lumber like that up the Creek road? I had thought that Buck was joking when he told me that; but now I knew for certain that he had meant what he said, and the mystery of the thing began to work on me like wine in the blood.

Well, I turned my shoulder on the temptation as firmly as I could; and I went about the morning calmly enough. After breakfast I sat in at a three-handed game, and about ten in the morning I had a hundred and fifty dollars stacked upon the table in front of me. I was in the middle of the neatest winning streak that I had ever started. The cards were for me. There was plenty of coin in that party, and I felt that I could drift my way to a year's holiday by noon.

But all at once I had to jump up from my chair and push all my winnings back into the game.

"Boys," said I, "there's your cash. I can't sit this game out, and I won't quit while you still want revenge. So long!"

They stared at me as though they thought that I was a madman; but I ran on up to my room, jerked my things together, and hurried out to the barn.

In five minutes more I was running Jupe up the trail. We came to the old Creek bridge—looking so rickety that I wondered how it could ever have stood the weight of the big wagon and its heavy load—but there was the track of the wheels, down the middle of it, and the great steel tires had sunk half an inch deep into the rotten surface.

I put Jupe at a hard run across that bridge and fanned him over the next hill with my quirt. After that I settled back in the saddle and took things easy, because I knew that I had committed myself so far on this expedition that I would not turn back.

It was later than noon before I sighted the dust cloud, however; for that team of mules knew how to step out on the road, and they could do four miles an hour when they had a fair chance. At least, so big Buck claimed for them; and I believe that he was right. They were the outwalkingest mules I ever saw.

But once I had the dust in sight, I was soon up with them. Buck turned around and gave me one dusty grin. Then he trudged on beside the wagon, and I jogged along behind.

I wasn't exactly contented. I felt that there was danger and bad danger ahead of us, some place. But I still couldn't figure what that danger might be.

"Hello!" says Buck suddenly. "Look at that buzzard, there, just out of rifle range. Queer how much sense them birds has, old-timer, eh? Know to ten yards just how far a rifle bullet will carry."

I looked up and spotted that buzzard. It was wheeling pretty low down, as buzzards fly.

"I dunno," said I. "Looks to me that a bullet would fan the feathers out of that piece of misery."

16

"Humph!" said Buck.

"Well," said I, "I'll show you, if you got any doubts."

I pulled my Winchester out of its sheath. It was a good gun. Any Winchester is a sweet rifle; but this was extra tight and handy, and it shot as straight as a ruled line—or straighter when you got to know its habits. I tipped up the barrel, studied the flight of the buzzard, and followed it for a couple of seconds.

"Hurry up!" said Buck. "It's climbing!"

It was climbing, well enough. You couldn't see a beat of the wings, but all at once that buzzard began to whirl around in its circle three times as fast as it had gone before. It was climbing fast, in the mysterious way that buzzards know. They may be things of horror to look at close up, but they're certainly things of wonder on the wing. And this black bit of mystery was fairly sliding off up into the heart of the sky. It was a long shot; but I got a good bead, and a pretty fair sense of the drift of the bird. Then I pulled the trigger.

"You see!" called Buck. "Out of range!"

"If I didn't hit that bird, I'm a liar," said I.

And just then the buzzard stopped sailing along and tumbled fast for the ground. It hit with a thump fifty yards away, but neither of us had any curiosity about taking a closer look at it.

Then I looked aside at Buck Logan; and I saw that he was trying to look calm, but that he was really swallowing a lot of exultation. His face had the look of a man who says, "I told you so."

Even if I had not smelled a rat long before, one glance at that expression of Logan's would have been enough to convince me that we were bound for a place where there would be a premium on straight shooting and quick thinking. He was very pleased that I had

17

brought that buzzard down, and I could see that the old rascal had been merely trying me out without asking me to show what I could do

DAGGETT VALLEY

IT WAS ABOUT A DAY AFTER THIS, THAT WE TURNED TO the left and headed through the hills over a road where the wheels sank deep and where the wagon stalled every couple of miles and the mules had to fight and struggle to get it rolling again.

I watched the course that we were taking, and all at once I yelled at Buck:

"We're heading for the Creek! We're going right straight for Daggett Creek!"

"Son," said he, "you talk sense; but why for shouldn't we be heading for Daggett Creek?"

"Why for shouldn't we? Why for should we, would be a lot more reasonable question to ask, I should say. Who would want to haul lumber to Daggett Creek— unless they're going to start up with a dude ranch there?"

"Son," said Buck, "you can keep on guessing until the time comes—which I hope that it will come to you easy, and not in a hard lump."

That was all he would say. But there we were, aimed across the white hills of the desert plumb in the direction of the Creek.

I said to Buck, "Tell me the truth. Some sucker thinks that he can strike gold there again!"

"Maybe he does and maybe he doesn't," said Buck.

"Leastwise," said I, "since I've rode this far into the deal with you, I think that you might open up and tell me what's what so far as you know."

"Kid," said Buck, "there's nothing I appreciate more than the way that you've kept yourself from pestering me with questions on this here trip. I thought that my tongue would ache just from saying, I don't know. But you've kept your face shut. Now I'll tell you why I ain't talked out more free and easy to you—and the reason is that although you're my pal, I've given my word that I won't talk no more than I have to."

"They've made you swear to keep things as dark as possible?"

"That's what they've done, though they must of knowed that they was taking a chance."

"They was," said I, "seeing that your wagon ain't any ghost wagon. If a blind man wanted to follow you, he would have an easy time of it."

"He would," said Buck; "but he would have to take along provisions for several days, I guess."

That was true, too. The best way to discourage anybody that started on that trail would just be to let him taste some of the length of the miles and the length of the hot days.

How the mules got through it I can't guess. I know that my Jupe hoss, which was about as tough as they come in any country, was fagged and almost done for. But those mules had grain twice a day from the sacks that big Buck Logan carried along with him. And every time he came to a suspicion of a run of water, Buck would stop the team and drench them down—sloshing the water over them for an hour at a time, because he said that that done them a lot of good.

He made three halts a day—in the mid-morning—a long one at noon—and another in the middle of the long afternoon. And Heaven knows how long a hot afternoon can be in the desert! Every time he halted he would strip every peg and strap of harness from the mules, and he would wash off the sweat from their shoulders and the backs of their necks where the heavy collars galled them; and then he would turn them loose to graze on whatever grass that they could find and to enjoy a roll and a mite of freedom, at least.

Of course it took a lot of time, and it cost him more work than you would ever guess, because he had to do it all himself. Those mules didn't appreciate the touch of any human being other than Buck, and I think he was proud of having such a string of man-eaters and wanted to keep them just that way.

But the way they ate up the miles, and the way they snaked that heavily loaded wagon through the drift sands was a caution. Half a dozen times we had to get out and shovel out trenches through the loose surface and down to the hard footing for them. But every other time they worked their own way out in a very scientific fashion.

They got thin; but they stuck to their jobs, and they were still in amazing good shape when the gray head of the leader turned through the little pass between the hills and we saw the green of the valley beneath us—Daggett Valley—and it never could have looked better, even to the gold rushers, than it did to us.

There was a boundary which you could cross in three steps, most of the way. On one side of the hills everything was dead and burned. And on the other side the sand hills showed you what they would grow when they had a fair chance to get a drink of water now and then; so that it was a pretty sight, I can tell you, with the grass growing as thick and as even and as crowded as though it had been planted.

Buck couldn't resist the temptation. He unharnessed his team right there; and we watched them break into those green fields and eat and eat, and then stop to roll, and then get up and eat again like gluttons. You couldn't of trusted a dry-fed horse with such fodder; he would of killed himself, sure. But a mule is different; it is too mean to do itself any real harm. Well, those mules feasted themselves full; and we sat down and drank in the beauty of the valley, and I'll tell you how soft we were. When a fat young buck stepped out of the I brush to watch the mules playing with one another, neither Buck Logan nor myself reached for a rifle. We just felt plumb peaceful.

And, for that minute, I forgot that I was riding into danger of some kind about which I knew nothing, as yet. However, things that begin well don't always have the best endings.

ON GUARD

WE DIDN'T MAKE ANY EFFORT TO FORGE AHEAD AGAIN that day. We rested, and the horse and mules rested. Bright and early the next morning, we started down the valley.

The sun was burning hot, but the minute we got among the trees everything was cool and pleasant. I never saw finer pines in my life.

We pushed up the old road which followed along beside the creek. I think we went about a mile when we heard the clinking of hammers very busy ahead of us; and, when the mules were given a halt and a breathing space, the trees were filled with echoes flying about as the hammers chattered away. It was almost like the noises that you wake up and hear in a town. I looked at Buck Logan.

However, he didn't choose to talk, and I wouldn't ask questions; but I knew that that was our goal—that place where men were busy building. And I was glad of it. There was something cheerful about the sound; it did you good to listen to it.

Then we started ahead again, and we came out from under the shadows of the big pines and into a clear stretch with only a scattering of trees here and there; and on a hillside near the creek was not a camp being built, but a big house.

It was a good, strong-built house, big enough to have maybe a dozen rooms in it; and I could guess that it must have been run up back in the days of the mining boom, when perhaps the creek looked good enough to one of the miners to be home all the year around.

Indeed, I think that some of those miners thought that the pay dirt would never give out. They got so many quick millions out of the surface dirt that they thought there had to be a continuation down into the rocks. It was too good to finish off with nothing—but, strangely, that was exactly what happened.

The gold was gutted out of the creek. Nothing was left but the bare rigs of the rocks and the big trees. In a single month the whole population drifted away. I had never known there was such a house as this up the creek. But, for that matter, there was a whole lot about the creek and the creek people that nobody ever knew for certain. For a couple of years a thousand things happened every day along that little run of water. There were enough murders and excitement of all kinds to fill a book every week. One thing piled on top of the other, and the heads of people were too filled to retain everything.

However, there was the house as big as life; and the clattering of the hammers came from inside of it. Out in front there was a litter of lumber and some homemade sawbucks, with a drift of yellow sawdust lying on the ground and sparkling almost like the glittering gold itself.

I didn't need more than that to explain everything. The last eight-mule load of lumber had gone to this same spot; and the carpenters were using up the last of it to fit up the inside of the house, while Buck Logan brought on more stuff to polish off the job. That was enough explanation for any man; I mean, that was enough surface explanation, though underneath the surface there was as much of a mystery as ever. Why people would want to come out here to the end of the world, beat me.

I soon learned that the two carpenters who had been so busily at work were Roger Beckett and Zack Morgan. And I learned, also, that it was to be my job to guard the house against intruders.

But how was I to go about guarding the place, since that was my duty?

I talked it over with big Buck Logan. My idea was that I should stand guard with guns at hand all day and only knock off for a short sleep at night. It would be hard work, but at the same time it would be some return for the high pay which I was getting. Buck listened to all I had to say, and then he simply smiled at me. He said that it showed my heart was right, but it showed that I was not thinking very straight.

How could I stand guard and shelter the whole house, and men working here and there all around the place, inside and outside? I could stand guard for a year and have a thousand men shot down around me from the shelter of the trees that overlooked the house on all sides.

Yes, that was very true; and I could see it, so I asked Buck to make his own suggestion. He had some, of course. There was never a man to beat Buck for suggestions; he had more ideas than an east wind has drops of rain.

He said that the main thing was for me to take it easy and have a good time.

"How can I sit around and take it easy," said I, "when I got the responsibility of the lives of three gents on my hands, and half a dozen murderers waiting out yonder— as you tell me there are—all ready to jump in and cut our throats."

Buck, he only smiled at me. He said, "Now, kid, don't go off half cocked, like this. Lemme tell you something that is true and darned true at that. Nobody can really work well until he can work happily, and the picture of you standing up and holding onto a gun all day long ain't a happy picture. I tell you what you do. You like hunting. Now what you should do is to make this a little hunting party. You can't have your eyes open all day and every day, and all night and every night. What I say is that you should just go out and look for game two or three times a day. And when you out regular for game, what always happens? The game is scared away. Well, kid, you can bet your boots that this two-legged game that we're talking about will be scared away, too—or at least, it will get dog-goned cautious. It will see signs of your tramping around this here place in a big circle. And it will make them pretty cautious.

"Now, what I'd suggest is that you go out about three times—and that you pick the times when folks generally

24

start out on deviltry. They go out in the morning, in the half light, to commit a lot of their crimes. And then they go out in the evening again. And besides that, of course, the time that they like best of all is the night. So I suspect that you'd better make a round in the mornings. Just loop around through the trees and zigzag so that you cover a couple of miles, keeping your eyes open all of the time. After that you take your time off and loaf along until the evening. And when the evening comes, you can make another trip, and the same some time during the night."

"Look here, Buck, you want me to go hunting at night?"

"I'm not asking you to hunt painters or coons," said Buck. "All I'm asking you to do is to ward off men from us; and if it's hard for you to see at night, it will be hard for them, too. I've an idea that you might have a lot more luck by night than you have by day."

This gave me something to think about; but after all it wasn't very hard to see that Buck, as usual, was pretty right. If I stood around with a gun all day long, what would I be except a mark for them to shoot at? But if I traipsed around through the forest in the evening and in the morning—that is to say, in the hunting times when all the beasts turn out in the woods—then it would be a good deal different. I might have luck.

I said, "Here's another little thing. Suppose I do come across somebody. What do I do?"

"Shoot!" said Buck. "Do I have to tell you that?"

"Shoot without no warning given?" says I.

"Why the devil should you give a warning?"

"Buck," says I, "I see that you got an idea that I'm just a butcher—which I ain't at all. Gents have got to be warned away from this valley before they're shot down,

25

and how is this to be arranged?"

"You're getting so particular, kid," said Buck, "that I dunno how you're goin' to be useful. What chance is there of anybody but crooks being stirring around here?"

"Not much chance," said I.

"Not one chance in a million," says Buck. "No, sir, and you know that. Who ever comes here to the Daggett Valley? Since the last of the gold was washed out, nobody comes here. You couldn't find a man here with a fine-toothed comb, except for the throat cutters that would like to get rid of the whole mob of us; so you're just talking through your hat uncommon loud and long, old son."

Well, there was a good deal in what he said. I thought it all over and I asked him how far the property ran that his boss—the folks that owned the old house on the hill—had a claim to in the valley. Buck pointed out the boundaries to me. It was a right smart piece of land, too, I can tell you.

I mapped out a regular beat for myself; and the first time I made the round, I spent a lot of time setting out the signs on which I had made up my mind. Those signs were flat, thin pieces of big board that I nailed onto trees where they could be seen easy, and on every board there was a few words in black paint:

PRIVATE PROPERTY
NO TRESPASSING

That was a sign that I could remember seeing and hating when I was a boy, because it had always looked sort of poisonous and mean, you know. But I figured that, with those signs up, there would be a lot more

26

excuse for me if I was to turn loose and pepper any strangers with powder and lead.

Buck, he let me do all of these things; and he agreed with me that it was the best way, and that it was making our game more aboveboard.

When I had finished putting up those signs and making my round, it was a good first day's work; and I was satisfied. I had stuck up about a dozen of those boards at all of the most prominent places, so that it would be pretty near impossible for folks that followed any of the natural trails toward the old house to fail to see those signs and read the warning that was on them. It was my duty, as near as I could make out. When I had done that I had another talk with Buck and Zack and Roger Beckett; and they all three agreed with me that from that time on, if I found any folks inside of the limits of those signs, I wouldn't have to stop and ask any questions. I could just haul off, and turn loose on them, and drop them if I could.

Besides, you see that the ground that I had fenced off with my warnings wasn't all of the property that belonged to the owner of the house, according to Buck Logan. It really wasn't more than a quarter or a fifth of the whole layout. But even so, it was big enough to make a stiff walk three times each twenty-four hours.

When I started making these rounds, things settled down at once, the two gents who were working at the repairing of the house, their nerves got more quieter; and you would think that I hadn't just started walking my rounds—you would think that I had fenced in that place with a wall of brass half a mile high.

THE BULLET FROM AMBUSH

I WAS GETTING READY FOR MY MORNING ROUND, several days later, when Buck Logan came down to me with a yellow face covered with wrinkles and shadows around his eyes, like a man who hasn't slept for weeks.

He said, "This is the big day, Doc."

"All right," said I. "If this is the big day, tell me what my part in it is to be."

"Get your Jupe hoss," said Buck, "and start drifting over toward the edge of the valley—the same road that we come in by. Go to that road and wait there till you see a covered wagon coming—an old-fashioned schooner. When you see that, ride up to it; and you'll find a little gent with a pointed gray beard sitting up driving, and along with him there'll be an old gent with long white hair and a tolerable pretty girl. You ride right up to them, and likely you'll have a gun held onto you, but don't be scared by that. It'll simply mean that the gent with the gray beard is playing safe. You go on up with your hands over your head and say that I sent you to him."

"What name shall I call him?" I asked.

"Names ain't any matter," said Buck Logan. "You don't need no names. Just give my name when you come up, and that'll be enough. But after that, mind that you don't do too much talking."

"All right," said I, "I can get along without talking. But what am I to do about the wagon and the folks that are in it?"

He said, "Your job is to get that wagon safe down through the trees and up the valley to the house, here.

28

You understand?"

"I understand," said I.

"And one of the main things is for you to get it here not before sunset. You hear?"

He counted out these things with a frown, stabbing at the palm of his hand with his forefinger.

I nodded. I couldn't make out why the wagon had to get to the old house after sunset time, but then that went along with a flock of other things that I didn't understand. I was getting used to being in a sort of a mist. I had, in all my time there, only learned that the chief one from whom we expected a lot of trouble, was named Grenville.

"Does Grenville want to stop that wagon?" I asked Buck.

He shook his head. "I dunno," said he. "Maybe Grenville does, and maybe he don't. Just what goes on inside of his head I can't make out; but, if he does suspect what those folks mean to us, he'll make the biggest try in the world to stop the rig. You understand?"

I nodded.

"I mean, he'll try killing," said Buck Logan.

"All right," said I. "The three of you stay here. I go out to bring in a wagon where there's a girl, a white-haired old man, and only one gent able to use guns—and him no youngster, as far as I can make out. I may have the whole gang of Grenville on my back!"

Buck nodded again. "Of course you may," said he; "there's no doubt about that. You're playing a dangerous game, to-day. But I'll tell you what, I'd almost as soon have your job at the wagon as have you away from the house this morning. If Grenville don't hit at you and the folks on the wagon, he's pretty apt to hit

29

at me and the boys that are here with me."

He seemed pretty serious about it, and Buck was not of a nature to take trouble any more serious than it had to be taken.

"All right, Buck," said I, "this is the beginning of the big play, then?"

"The beginning of the big play," he said, still as solemn as an owl.

"So long!" says I.

"So long!" says Buck, and turned on his heel.

So I went and got my Jupe hoss and rode down the valley.

I was so glad that the misery was gonna be over, danger or no danger, that I could have sung; and I did sing, as I went ramping along, as though there was not the least mite of danger in the world from Grenville and his clan.

This was the way I was feeling then—pretty proud and pretty gay—as I worked my way down through the woods, keeping to the old wagon trail and not making any particular effort to keep Grenville or any of his lookouts from spotting me.

When I look back to it, I wonder how any man could of been so plumb foolish as I was, when I started out. As if I hadn't been warned enough. No, you would think I had never been in that valley before, and that I didn't know there was such a person as Grenville in the whole wide world.

Well, we came to the place on the trail where there had been a bridge; but the bridge that crossed the old gully had busted down, long ago, and the wreckage of the wagon that had busted it down lay there in the hollow. The heavy ironwork of the wagon, that hadn't been washed away in the spring freshets, had lodged

30

among the rocks. The trail itself had swung aside, instead of rebuilding the wrecked bridge. The trouble had happened, I suppose, along toward the end of the mining days when it was hardly worth while repairing the road.

Anyway, the road dipped to the side and across the gulch at a slant; and just as we got to the middle of the crossing, while I was watching the ground ahead of me, Jupe stopped and whirled to the side. I thought the old fool was refusing on account of a little patch of water, an inch or so deep, that lay in front of us. So I cursed him and give him the spur—but, instead of straightening out, he just threw up his head with a snort; and, as he threw it up, a gun banged from the thicket, and the bullet that was meant for my brain bashed through Jupe's.

STALKING THE STALKER

AT LEAST, POOR JUPE DIED WITHOUT PAIN. HE FELL SO sudden and complete that I didn't have time to free my feet from the stirrups.

Also, I think that the quickness of that fall saved my life a second time. That fellow in the bushes was shooting as straight as he was shooting fast. One bullet combed past my head as Jupe fell, and another spattered dirt in my face as I rolled out of the saddle along the ground. That roll carried me within twisting distance of the brush, and I pitched myself into it just as a fourth bullet came whining for me.

I knew, as I crawled through those bushes, that only fate and Jupe had saved me. And kneeling there in the brush, handling my guns, I knew, too, that in five

31

minutes either I would be dead for sure, or the gent that had tried to murder me would be eating dirt.

I started straight for him. Yes, I was so mad that I went smashing and crashing through the brush, aiming right for the spot from which he had done the shooting—as though he must have used up his bullets, or as though I couldn't be killed with powder and lead!

Anyway, my wits came back to me before I had gone very far. I stopped on the edge of a little depression that couldn't be very far away from the spot where the other gent had laid for me. There was a part of a rotten stump lying on the group in front of me, and I kicked that stump so that it rolled along down the slope and come to rest in the brush straight ahead of me. There it lay, and it had made a sound a good deal like that which a man makes in charging wild, through the woods.

So I thought if the other gent really was near, the noise of that rolling stick might make him think I had ducked down into the brush at the bottom of that dip of ground.

Leastwise, if he was thinking that, there was nothing to keep me from taking him from behind.

I went slithering along as soft as I was able to work, and thanking Heaven for the breeze which come rustling and talking through the tops of the trees. That wind made about enough sound to drown out all the noise I was making. So I worked myself in a circle that brought me through a thick standing hedge of young poplars.

And then my heart jumped into my throat; for there he was, stretched out along the ground and turned away from me, with his rifle at the ready, trained on something before him and beneath him. I knew he was searching the hollow into which I had rolled the bit of stump.

I raised up easy and stepped through the trees. I didn't want to take no advantage of him; and so I figured that if I put my Colt into the holster and called out a warning to him, it would make about an even thing of it—his rifle against the surprise that I was giving him.

I did just that. I sneaked my revolver back into the holster; but just as I did that, something seemed to pop into his head and make him uneasy, because all at once he lifted up his head and stiffened all through his body.

"You houn' dog!" I snarled at him through my teeth.

I was thinking of the way that poor old Jupe had died for me—and just then it looked to me as though no man's life was more than enough to be paid down for that little old cutting hoss of mine.

When he heard my voice, he pitched himself right around and snatched his gun to his shoulder. I was half of a mind that, when he heard a voice like that behind him, he would stick up his hands, but there wasn't any quit in that man. He started for me like I was nothing at all, and almost before I could wink, the long barrel of that rifle was flashing at my eyes.

I yanked out my Colt. I didn't have time to take any aim or draw any bead. It was just a case of a snapshot from the hip, in case I wanted to get in something before he planted me with an aimed bullet; so I fired from the hip the instant I had flopped my Colt out.

The shot hit the gravel just in front of him and brought out a yell and a gasp. His rifle went off, but the bullet rattled through the branches, a long distance away from me. He jumped to his feet and threw his hands across his face.

He was blinded a bit. And, instead of shooting him down, I thought that it might be a pretty good thing if I closed in on him and took him a prisoner—because then he could act as a sort of hostage for us and maybe keep Grenville from trying to murder us from behind the brush.

So I ran in at him, full of this new idea.

It would have been easy, if he had really been blinded, but he wasn't. He saw me coming and wrenched at his Colt. He got it out of the holster, but just then I reached for him with my fist and managed to hit his jaw. He went down on his back with a thump and a grunt, and the Colt clanged on the rocks.

No, he wasn't done fighting yet. As he lay there he kicked out and knocked my feet out from under me. Down I fell right on top of him, and, believe me, it was like falling on the top of a wild cat. He was just a mite faster than chain lightning and a little bit stronger than a tiger. But as I fell, I got a throat hold. He whanged at my face, and he tore at my hands; he was so strong that in half an instant he was on top of me, and I was under him. But before he could use that advantage, my grip told on him. His face blackened, his eyes turned up in his head, and he went limp and soft.

I rolled him off and threw a handful of water in his face from my canteen. And I saw him come to by steps and stages, and you might say, just pulling himself together by degrees, so I sat up and shook myself to see where I was hurt.

I can tell you that had been an exciting little whirl, while it lasted; but, when I had gathered myself together, there was the other chap sitting up and beginning to blink at me. I blinked at him, too; and I was terrible surprised by what I seen, because here was the red hair and the fine, handsome features which I had been told 'Red' Grenville had.

"Look here," said I, "are you any relation of Henry

34

Grenville?"

"Perhaps I am," says he, and he began to brush the leaves and the dirt out of his hair, as cool as you please.

"Well," said I, "I was half of a mind that I would take you along with me alive. Now that I see that you come of decent blood, and that you should know better than to shoot from cover—why, curse you, I got a mind to plant a slug between your eyes and leave you here."

He smiled straight into my face. There was a ton of nerve in him.

"How long," says he, "have gun fighters like you been in the habit of talking about fair play and not shooting from cover?"

It was a facer for me. I listened, and I wanted to shoot him full of holes, I can tell you; but I managed to control myself—I don't know how. I said to him:

"I'll tell you, old-timer, that wherever you've learned your stuff about me, you've learned it wrong."

"Bah!" says he. "How many men have you shot down from behind a wall? And how many have you shot through the back?"

I let out a yell, it made me so mad. "You young fool!" I shouted at him. "If I shot men from behind, why didn't I shoot you down that way—when I had the chance to take you helpless from behind, just now—instead of giving you a little more than a fair break for your life?"

"Why—" said he, and then he stuck.

In the excitement of things happening so fast and so close together, I suppose he had not had a chance to think things over exactly as they happened; but now he frowned and looked as though this think he had just thought about made him a little unhappy.

"I don't care about that," he said, rather sullenly. "The fact is that Henry has told us that you're worthy to

35

be hunted like a dog—and that's my excuse—and that's excuse enough."

"Henry Grenville told you that?"

"Yes," says he. "I suppose that you'll call him a liar?"

I didn't answer. I seen that there was no use in arguing with him over a thing like this. The main thing was that I had a brother of Henry Grenville that I could use as a sort of hostage. And I could just about swear that Henry would stop the shooting from behind trees, from this point on.

"Stand up!" says I. "Stand up and get ready to march."

"I'm ready here," said he. "I'd as soon pass out here as anywhere, but I don't think that I'll march for you."

FORWARD MARCH

IT TOOK ME A MOMENT OR SO TO UNDERSTAND THAT this young fool had it fixed in his mind that I was going to murder him before I got through.

When I had digested that idea for a minute, I looked him in the eye; and I said, 'Grenville, what's your first name?"

"Lawrence," says he, as cool as ever.

"Lawrence," says I, "lemme tell you that your brother may be a blooming angel so far as truth telling may be concerned, and I may be the worst black rat in the world; but the fact is, old-timer, that I ain't going to murder you. Not to-day, that is—maybe to-night I'll cut your throat, and may be to-morrow I'll shoot you through the back; but to-day, I've took a fancy to letting you live, y'understand? And if you care to eat a couple of more squares, you'll buck up and do what I tell you.

36

But, if the next few hours ain't got nothing in store for you, why, I'll polish you off right here and now."

He listened to me as though I was speaking a foreign language that he didn't understand. But finally he said, "Well, I'll let you have it your own way. Where do you want me to march to?"

"Where I tell you," said I; and I guided him back through the woods to the spot where my poor Jupe hoss lay.

Says I, "This is what you done, Larry, my boy."

"He threw his head up," says this cool cucumber. "Otherwise you'd be lying there, and he'd be eating grass—with an empty saddle."

I couldn't help admiring this young fool of a boy, in a way. Nobody but a courageous idiot, that didn't care whether or not he lived, would talk like this to a man who had the drop on him. But it was plain to be seen that courage ran pretty thick in the blood of the Grenvilles.

I said, "Yes, you meant that bullet for me; but maybe while you was shooting at me you murdered something that was a lot better than me—if you admit that a hoss can be better than a man."

"Ah," says he, with a quick look aside at me, "don't I admit that, though? I do! And I've known the horses—and the men." And he laughed with a sudden sort of enthusiasm.

I began to take more and more of a liking for him. Even if he had been taught to shoot from behind trees—well, there was something decent about him in spite of that.

"Look here, Grenville," said I, "this here Jupe hoss was the best cutting hoss I ever rode on. And he was the gamest hoss on the trail that you ever seen."

37

"He's a pretty little rabbit," said Grenville.

"Rabbit?" says I. "That rabbit, you bonehead, would carry two hundred pounds at a canter nearly all day long. He's stood between me and a rotten sort of a death more times than once. Do you think that the fact that he died for me makes me feel any easier about it, or any kinder to you, Grenville?"

All the time that I said this he wasn't looking at the horse, he was looking at me; and when I finished, he said, "Willis, if I'd been you—well—Larry Grenville would be a dead man."

"Well," said I, "there was never a time from the beginning of the world when shooting from behind brush done any real good. It's got me a dead hoss, and I think that you're decent enough to have it give you a few bad nights during the rest of your life. Now help me get the saddle off of him."

He started to work without a word. We stripped everything off of Jupe, and then he pointed to a tower of loose rock that heaved up on the bank just above the spot where Jupe lay in the hollow. I took that for a pretty good hint; and we heaved away side by side until that tower toppled, and three or four tons of rock went crashing and sliding over the spot where Jupe was and buried him from sight complete.

After that it was easier to go along on my trail, but Larry was a pretty silent boy for the rest of the way. He didn't have nothing to suggest, and his head hung pretty low.

Suddenly he broke out, as we turned onto the up slope that pointed toward the edge of the valley, "Henry was all wrong about you, Willis."

"I'll tell you why," said I. "I would be a lot more use to him dead than living. You can write that down for

38

facts. Step out, kid; I'm overdue."

We swung down that trail for another couple of miles, until we come to the edge of the green; and there was the whiteness and the oven heat of the desert before us.

"What d'you aim to do with me?" asked Larry Grenville.

"I aim to keep you with me," I said, "as a sort of a promise that while you're here, Henry won't try his hand at any more Indian fighting. Is that fair?"

He nodded right away. "That's fair," he said.

"And if you try to break away—why, I'll treat you the way you treated my little old Jupe hoss. Is that square?"

"The squarest thing in the world," said he. "And darn it, Willis, I feel as though this was a black day in my life." And he went on with a frown on his face, thinking hard all of the time.

We kept on for about another hour, and then I made a halt on the edge of one of the low sand hills where we could get at something that served as an excuse for shade—I mean, we sat down in the skeleton shadow of a group of Spanish daggers. And we let the perspiration come trickling down our faces while I started off to the horizon across the flashing and shining heat waves of the desert.

By what big Buck Logan had said, I had guessed that I would find the covered wagon coming over the hills early in the morning; but it was pretty near to noon before I saw a little spot of white against the sky, like a cloud brushing across the face of the earth.

"What's that?" asked Larry.

"More trouble for your brother is what it looks like to me," I told him.

He stared and stared, but he wouldn't ask any more questions.

Then I said, "Look here, Larry, do you know the thing that brought your brother up here to Daggett Valley?"

"Of course," says he, with a quick look to the side at me.

"Is it worth the trouble that he's taking?" I asked.

"That all depends," said Lawrence Grenville. "The money might be worth the trouble to him, but the fun would be worth the trouble to me."

"And do the gents that are working for Henry figger on getting in on a split of the loot?"

"They work by the day," said Larry; "but why do you ask me this stuff?"

"I wanted to see," said I, "how big a business man he was."

In the meantime the dust cloud was floating across the hills toward us; and now that cloud lifted a little, and I could see through the film of it the outlines of the arched back of the wagon, and then four animals that was pulling the load. It couldn't be a very heavy load, because they came along at a fast walk; and they did not stop at the inclines, as Buck Logan had stopped his mule team when he worked our way across the same trail.

Now the thing came closer and closer. It was one of those old-fashioned wagons such as they used to use, in the gold days, for making voyages around on the prairie and across the barren desert.

Grenville stood up and peered at them. "It looks odd," said he. "What are they doing with one of those clumsy old things?"

"Why," said I, "maybe they're on the track of the same trouble that brought your brother into Daggett Valley. Come on down with me and we'll hail them."

40

He stepped out from the shadow along with me, but as we got down into the trail there was a shout from in front of us. I saw the mules stop, and I saw a rifle leveled at us in the hands of a man with a gray, pointed beard.

Buck was a true mind reader, right enough!

MEETING THE PRAIRIE SCHOONER

"YOU'VE WALKED US INTO A BUNCH OF LEAD," SAID Larry Grenville. "I thought you were a friend of this gang?"

It was a fact. The gray-bearded fellow looked pretty wicked behind that rifle of his, but we hoisted up our hands and walked in to talk to the tiger face to face. When we got to the heads of the leading span of mules he stopped us again.

"Now who are you?" he asked me.

"I am Doc Willis," said I.

He snapped. "Where's your horse?"

"Dead," said I. "Dead where?"

"Dead in Daggett Valley," said I. "And you walked on here?"

"Yes."

"With good news or bad?"

"With no news worth talking about," said I.

"Keep your hands up," said he; "and let your partner back up a bit."

I told Grenville to do as he was ordered; and he backed out of the way, while the gray-beard climbed down from his seat and came up to me. As soon as he was on the ground he didn't look half so impressive as sitting down. He was one of those short-legged, long-waisted fellows. I suppose he didn't stand taller than me; but seated, he looked like a six-footer, at least. He came toward me with a sort of a wabble in his stride, because he was very bow-legged.

"Now," said he, speaking quietly when he came up to me, "tell me where you stand; and you don't have to shout it."

I said, "Buck Logan sent me out here to meet you."

"To meet who?" said he.

"A girl, a white-haired old gent, and a gray-bearded fellow in a covered wagon."

"And what names did Buck tell you they wore?"

"Buck told me no names."

He frowned again at this. "What did Buck mean by that?" he growled.

"You can answer that better than me," said I.

"What's your job with Buck?" he asked me.

"Me?" said I. "I'm the chore boy and I carry water for the real men."

"Don't talk smart," says the gray-bearded gent. "That will win you nothing with me. I asked you what you were doing for Buck."

"Fifty dollars' worth a week," said I.

He canted his head a little to one side.

"Buck is paying big wages, then," said he.

"That's all in the way you look at it," I told him. "It looked good to me at first, but now it looks fairly small."

"Humph!" says he.

"Humph!" says I.

"Bear a civil tongue in your head," says he. "Do you know who I am?"

42

"I don't give a darn who you are," says I. "A gray beard ain't a title, not in this part of the world."

I thought that that would get a flare out of him, but instead he let a smile come halfway on his lips.

"You don't get fifty a week for that sort of talk," said he.

"No," said I, "I get fifty a week for riding herd on the rest of them and keeping the chills away."

"Humph!" says he. "Then you're the killer that Logan was to try to hook up with?"

"Am I the killer?" says I, getting madder and madder. "Well, in my part of the country folks ain't so fond of calling me that."

"Oh," says he. "I'll be polite to you, if that's what you want. And what was your name again?"

"Willis," says I; and, as I look him over, I feel that there ain't anybody that I ever met that I liked less than this fellow. He was about as cold as ice; and his eyes had a way of going snicker-snack, right through you and finding out what was on your insides.

"Willis," says he, "you came out to guard us into the valley, I suppose; but you don't know who I am?"

"I don't," said I. "And I don't—"

"Leave that out," he broke in, as cool as ever, but smiling a little again, "but you might as well know me now. I'm Alston."

"Alston?" says I. "Then I suppose that the old white-headed gent on the seat, yonder, is Carberry?" For I'd heard some mention of a gent by the name of Carberry being mixed up in this affair.

He gave a start and a blink. 'Carberry? Why, don't you know—" began Alston.

Then he stopped himself and stared at me, like a man would at a fellow who said that the earth was flat.

43

"No," said I, "I never had the pleasure of meeting up with Carberry. Who is he? President?"

"Maybe you'll be ready to vote for him in that job," says the gray-beard, "before you get through with this game. Now, who is the fellow who's with you?"

"Don't you like him?" says I.

"Don't be sassy, Willis," says Alston; "tell me who he is. I have a right to know, because I won't take another step into the valley without knowing who I have along with me."

"All right," I replied to him, "I don't mind telling you that he is the gent that dropped my Jupe hoss."

He took another quick look at young Larry Grenville, and then he took a long look at me and seemed to be really seeing me for the first time.

"The man who killed your horse—how?"

"From behind a tree."

"And you got him?"

"There he is!"

"But you didn't scalp him, eh?"

"Alston," said I, getting madder and madder, "whether you like the looks of me, or I like the looks of you ain't a matter of any importance; but what really counts is that I ain't a killer, and that I won't be talked to like one. And I want you to write that down in red letters and never to forget it. I don't kill gents for the sake of keeping my hand in."

"Very hot!" says Alston, nodding at me, and looking me over like I was a horse or a dog. "All right. I won't rub your hair the wrong way. Only—what do you intend to do with the man? What's his name?"

"Grenville," said I.

I thought that might get a little more attention from him, but I didn't expect it to make him stagger. He reached out and gripped my arm, and there was a lot more power in that hand of his than I had thought. By the feel of that grip of his, I peeled ten years off my guess of his age. No, he wasn't as old as the gray beard had made him look—not by a long ways.

"Henry Grenville!" says he. "That's not possible! And yet—I can half remember the face; and there is the red hair. Good heavens, Willis, if that's Grenville, our troubles are all ended."

"Are they?" I snarled at him, because I hated him every minute more and more. "Well, he's Grenville, all right, but his first name isn't Henry."

"Not Henry? The devil!"

I told him that the name of this fellow was Lawrence, but here Alston pricked up his ears again. He said that next to having Henry himself, this capture was best, because with it, we could tie the hands of Henry himself pretty effectually. He said that we would put Larry into the wagon, and that he, Alston, would keep guard over him, while the old chap drove the wagon along the road and I went on ahead to scout for trouble.

"Because," said Alston, "when Henry finds out that his brother has disappeared, he'll come shouting for trouble; and when he starts to make trouble, he's very apt to finish the job that he begins."

Then he took me back toward the wagon.

"Don't mind the old boy," says he. "He's pretty safe and sane, today. But I had a rocky time with him on Wednesday."

While he led me up toward the seat, we took another look for Larry. I hadn't been watching him very close, because it would be hard for him to get away. He had no gun with him, now; and, if he tried to break away, it would be dead easy for me to pick him off before he had got very far through that loose surface of sand.

Well, there hadn't been any idea in the mind of Larry of escaping. And now there he was, leaning beside the driver's seat, as calm as you please, smoking away at a cigarette and making conversation with the old fellow and the girl.

They made a picture, I can tell you, Larry Grenville, almost handsomer than any man had a right to be, standing there with his head thrown back, and the girl leaning above him and laughing down to him—and she prettier than any I had ever seen. The old chap, he sat back with his hands folded in his lap, smiling at Larry, and smiling at the girl, but with his eyes mostly fixed far off on the horizon, and his smile not meaning a great deal of anything. I could see that he was only about half or a quarter with us. Sickness and death had begun at the top, with him. And when I come up close and looked up into his thin, kind, old face, with the white hair streaming down around it, a wave of pity come over me which I've never recovered from to this day. I would have cut off an arm to make the old chap smile with a bit of life in his face.

Alston did the introducing in a pretty free and easy way.

"Lou Wilson," says he to the girl, "this is Willis. And," says Alston, "Doc, this is William Daggett."

I had thought there couldn't be many more surprises crowded into this day of my life. From the beginning right straight, there had been something happening every little while; but this was the crown of everything. For here was a name that had passed from reality and become part of a story, all through that section of the West. Here was the man that had struck gold on the creek. Here was the man that had struck the gold and

46

started the rush that crowded Daggett Creek, in a little while, with miners gouging through the earth to get rich. Here was the man, too, who had built the house on the hill that Buck had been working so hard to get into shape and freshen up and make like new.

And what was he? Why, the man that had done all of these things and made so much history, he was just a hollow husk. Once there had been a man inside of him, but now he was like a light that has burned low and is about to flicker out. And there was a flicker in the blue eyes of Daggett, as he smiled down at me—a quiet, sad, feeble sort of a light that made me almost sorry that I was alive.

"I'm proud to know you, Mr. Daggett," said I. "I've just been up in the valley where you—"

Here Alston stepped heavily on my foot.

But I hadn't made any break, so far as the old fellow was concerned. He just smiled and nodded at me and said, "Exactly! Exactly! And what a world it is, Mr. Wallis! What a world it is, Mr. Wallis!"

Even my name, which he'd heard half a minute before, he couldn't remember; and now his old blue eyes wandered off to find their favorite spot on the horizon.

LOU TALKS

ALSTON WANTED FOR ME TO HANDLE THE TEAM WHILE he watched Grenville in the wagon, and I said that I would; but not being used to handling four reins, I jumped up onto the rear leader and started to guide the team that way, reining the leaders the way I wanted them to go. But before we had rolled a hundred yards, somebody yipped on the far side of the off leader; and there was Lou, sitting sidewise on the off leader, and laughing at me, as easy and as companionable as you please.

I looked back to the wagon, and it amused me a good deal to see it bothered two of them a lot to watch the girl out there riding the mule at my side. It bothered young Larry Grenville, for one. And it bothered the gray-beard, too.

Lou hooked a thumb back over her shoulder.

"How did you ever happen to pick up with this gang of thugs?" said she.

"I was gonna ask you the same thing," said I.

"You was?" says Lou. "Well, I asked you first. Let's have what you got to say for yourself."

"Suppose," said I, "that you was a cow-puncher."

"Yes," says she.

"And suppose that you was out of a job, and wondering what gang you would pick on with next, and suppose the most you ever got for riding range was about forty bucks a month—"

"I know," said she.

"And then a gent drives by with an eight-mule load of lumber and he says. 'Come along with me and get your fifty bucks a week, and all you got to do is to ride herd on a couple of gents that I've got at work'—why what would you have said, Lou?"

"I would of said, 'Come take me quick, before you get a chance to change your mind.' What did you say, Doc?"

"I told him that I didn't want his game, and I let him roll on out of my sight; but after he was gone, I just couldn't stand it. Along in the middle of the day I went pelting along after him, and so—here I am, still riding

48

around in circles, and still in the dark."

"In the dark," she says, with her husky voice suddenly barking at me. "Did I hear you straight?"

"You heard me straight," I told her.

She straightened around so that she could look fairly and squarely at me. It was a strange thing, but when you faced Lou you could see the thoughts working in her eyes. Not just what they were, of course; but you could see her eyes brighten and darken, and you could see the color change from blue to gray and back again. I never seen such a pair of eyes in my life, and neither did any other man.

"Say, Doc," said she, "maybe you're an innocent, poor, young boy that's being dragged into this dirty deal sort of against his will."

"Maybe I am not," says I, laughing back at her when I saw her drift. "I ain't asking you for any of your pity, Lou."

"Thanks," says she. "That's one strain off my mind. But what do you mean by saying that you're riding around in the dark?"

"Ain't that plain English?" said I.

"Don't get huffy," says she. "I'm not riding you."

"You give a pretty good imitation of it. What are you driving at?"

"You ain't a baby. How could they ring you in with your eyes closed?"

"I'm a hired man, here, not a boss."

That seemed to surprise her.

"If they get in gents like you for the hired-man parts," said she, "this is quite a show—bigger, even, than I thought."

"And how big did you think?" I asked her.

"Oh, I don't know. Hundreds of thousands, I

49

suppose."

"What makes you suppose that?"

"Are you pumping me?"

"Not a bit more than you want to talk, Lou."

She nodded. It was easy to see that she had her eyes open all the time, but she didn't want to be hostile.

"I don't see any reason why you and me shouldn't be friends, Doc."

"None in the world," said I. "I'm keeping a tight hold on myself to keep from being too friendly too quick."

She frowned at me. "What might you mean by that?"

"I'll explain later, when I know you better," I told her.

"Well," said Lou, "have you told me all you know?"

"Oh, no," said I; "I don't mind letting you know what I've gathered. It ain't much."

"Fire away," said she.

"Well, all I know is that Buck Logan brought me up here."

"I've heard about him," said she. "What sort is he?"

"Square," said I. "A big gent, slow-speaking, usually—and honest, I think."

"But you ain't sure?"

"I'm sure of nothing in this game."

"Not even of me?"

I looked into those wonderful, queer, changing eyes of hers. "Not even of you."

I thought that this might anger her a little, but there was nothing soft about that girl.

"All right," said she, "that doesn't make me mad. It's gonna be pretty easy to talk to you, Doc. So you don't even know Buck Logan?"

"I don't. I thought I did. I still feel mighty friendly toward him. But lately I've got the idea that this

50

business means a lot more to him than any friendship would."

"No friend would stand between him and the cash he expects to get out of the deal?"

"That's right. That's about the way I figure it."

"Is Logan inside of the deal?"

I thought it over for a minute; then I said, "It seems to me that Logan must know about as much as anybody. But I'm not sure even of that. He may be only a hired man, as far as I know. I'm sure of nothing."

"Go on," says she.

"Well, then, I know that up there in the valley there's Henry Grenville, a gentleman with education, and all that. And he's got a crowd of gun fighters with him, and he's gunning to get something out of the deal."

"Is that all you know about him?"

"That's about all. Then there's something about the old Daggett house. Do you know what it is?"

"The Daggett house?" said Lou. "No. What has a house to do with it?"

"A lot. I see that there's a lot you don't know, Lou; but, take it from me, when this thing is opened up and explained, the old Daggett house will have a lot to do with the explanation. At least, that's the way Buck Logan and his crew are expecting it to happen. But they ain't sure. I can see that Buck ain't sure. He's working in the dark, and he don't know just where he's going. And I can see the worry of it in his face all the time."

She nodded, thinking of everything that I had to say.

"Then, behind this thing, or mixed up in it I don't know how, there's you and old Daggett. You can tell me something about that. Then somewhere in the yarn there is Carberry—"

"What Carberry?"

51

"The bandit."

"Carberry, the bandit? Oh, he's dead a long time ago," said Lou."

"Dead!" I shouted at her. "Why, Lou, then his ghost is back in this business and using his hand somewhere and in some way. I know that for certain."

"Go on," said Lou; "this is pretty interesting."

"I've got to the end of my rope," said I. "I used to think, at first, that there was something hidden in the bottom of the house; but, if that was the case, I suppose they would tear the old place to pieces and find out what it was. Anyhow, the thing they're looking for must be so big that it couldn't be hidden in a nutshell; even if it was pure solid gold, it would have to take up a good deal of room."

"Why," said Lou, "maybe they're looking for some sort of a paper."

"Humph!" said I. "That sounds a good deal too much like a book to convince me."

"May be it does," she admitted; "but we got to try everything, if we want to hope to hit on the right trail, here."

I admitted that that was right. Then I told her how the old house was being fixed up, and she wondered at that no end. She couldn't make head nor tail out of it, because she agreed with me that nobody would fix up a big house like that just to live in, with Daggett Creek so far from the rest of the world. And what the hidden purpose could be was a sticker.

It was good to talk these things all over with her, because she was as smart as a whip; and she thought three thoughts while I was thinking one.

Then I asked her what she knew about Alston, because he seemed to be as high up in the deal as anybody.

She thought for a minute before she answered, and then she said, "Well, I'll tell you about Alston. I've known some crooks in my day. I've known cattle rustlers and yeggs. Dad was free and easy, and he never cared who came and tapped at his door and asked for a meal and a place to sleep. I've seen some pretty hard cases around our house; but I'll tell you what—the lowest, the meanest, the sharpest, the smartest, and the wickedest of the lot is that gambler, Alston!"

I sort of knew beforehand just what she would say, somehow. I'd felt all of those things about him.

I couldn't help breaking out, "It's pretty good to hear you say that, Lou; because it's easy to see that he don't feel the same way about you as you do about him."

"He wants me to marry him; and he expects that I will, when I see how rich this deal will make him. You understand? But I'll be dead before I ever marry him. You can lay your money on that bet."

Well, that was about the best news I'd ever heard.

TROUBLE AHEAD

I TOOK A WHILE TO DIGEST WHAT SHE'D JUST TOLD ME, and I felt so happy that I couldn't help slapping a mule on the hip and singing out at a rabbit that came hopping across the wagon trail.

"Only," said I at last, "that don't tell me how you was rung in on this deal."

"The reason is back in a bank," said the girl.

"Money?"

"Nothing but. That's why I'm here—and a good fat stake!"

"I hope so!" I told her.

"Twenty-five hundred iron men is what I corralled before I would go along in the party," said Lou.

And I blinked at her. "Why, Lou," said I, "it seems to me that old Alston would hardly pay that much for less than a murder."

"It looks that way, don't it?" said Lou. "And now I'll hand you a surprise. He's giving me that money and a lot more, if the deal works, and all for the sake of what?"

"I couldn't guess," said I.

"All for wearing a funny old dress! Can you beat that?"

No I couldn't beat that; and I was perfectly willing to tell her so.

"All right," said Lou, "but that's the fact, strange though you may think it."

I just looked at her.

"Do you believe me?"

"Lou," said I, "I don't know you well enough to tell you how many kinds of a liar I think you are."

She wasn't mad. She just put back her head and laughed. "Maybe you're partly right, too," said she; "but that's my story, and that is what I've got to stick to."

"Is that part of the bargain with Alston?"

"Alston? No, he'd probably poison you, if he knew that I'd told you even this much."

"Who is Alston?"

"Alston," says Lou, "is a gent that done what ain't possible."

"How do you mean?"

"In the old days, you know how the gamblers used to come down to the mining camps and cheat the boys out of their gold dust?"

54

"I've heard about that; and I've seen some of it, of course."

"Well, there's a good old saying that there was never a crooked gambler that didn't go on the rocks sooner or later?"

"Yes."

"Some of them got cleaned out at cards, when they met up with a worse crook than themselves. Some of them got stabbed in the back, and then some of them was shot down in fair fights and—"

"That's right, and I've seen it happen."

"But sooner or later, they all go; and their money goes, too, because it comes through their hands too easy to stick, you see?"

"All right," said I. "That's all a fact. But what has that to do with Alston?"

"Well, I'll tell you. He's the exception to the rule. He's the one old-time gambler that stayed with the game and that beat it. When he was gambling, he took every chance and played it big—big and crooked, I mean to say. He worked cards, and he worked dice. He knew how to fix up a crooked set of horse races and get the money out of the Indians, even. He knew how to salt up a claim very fine and stick a poor sucker with it. He knew all sorts of things; but, most of all, he was good at the dice, they tell me. He made money out of everything; and, finally, he had the nerve to draw back out of the game that he was in and go East and settle down where he could pretend to be respectable. That was the way with this here Alston."

"And now this game has brung him out of his shell?"

"That's it! He's got plenty of money. He's living easy. He's showed me a flock of pictures of his horses, and his dogs, and his house, and all of that. He's terribly proud of it; and it's a pretty good place, right enough. But this deal was big enough for the hopes of what he could make in it to bring him out West; and so here he is, and he thinks he'll win—though something tells me that he's taking a long, long chance."

"What makes you think that?"

"Why, for one thing, he told me that he never had this idea at all, until he seen me."

That staggered me.

"Until he seen you, Lou?" I gasped at her.

"I was in Denver with an uncle of mine. He went to Denver on a trip. And he seen me there, and hunted me up, and got to know my uncle—just so that he could have a chance to talk to me."

"When was that?"

"Last year."

"Been working on this deal ever since?"

"He said that he couldn't do a thing unless I would promise to work with him. And finally he came across with enough money to make me do what he wanted. And here I am, but that's not the only reason. There's old William Daggett, too. I know that poor old fellow is going to be leaned upon a lot by Alston, and you can see for yourself that Mr Daggett ain't to be depended upon. He's only about half here; and the other half is away off—nobody can tell where."

That was right enough.

"And still," said I, "Alston looks like a winner, to me."

"Sure," said Lou. "He says himself that he wasn't a gambler. He was just a gold digger, but he used cards and such things instead of a pick and shovel and got a lot more of the yellow stuff. He wouldn't be in this deal unless there was a fine big chance that he would win

56

with it."

I looked back into the wagon; and there was Alston sitting steady, with his eyes burning at me, and a bit in front of him was Larry Grenville, looking at me about as mean as old Alston was doing.

No, Alston didn't look like a loser—neither did young Grenville; and the two of them worried me a good deal.

"All right," said I to Lou. "There is one pretty sure thing. If Alston is in the deal, it's a crooked one."

"Maybe, and maybe not," said Lou. "I'll think about that when the time comes," and she began to laugh in her husky, careless way. I liked her fine, but she was still a puzzle to me.

I had something to think about besides the stuff of which we had been talking, pretty soon.

While Lou and me exchanged the little mites of information that we had to give, we had been pushing through miles of sand and passed the green border line just as the sun begun to turn red-gold before falling behind the western mountains. We slid down the first slope; and the leader just brought me over the tip of the next hill—the last hill before we dipped down into the long valley slope—and I had a glimpse, far ahead of me, of a horseman pushing his horse behind a clump of trees.

I didn't ask any questions. I had seen a man, a rifle, and a hoss; and I'd been in Daggett Valley long enough to know that that combination was apt to mean pretty ugly business before many hours had rolled by.

I popped off of the mule, and I ran back beside the driver's seat.

I said, "Chief, there's one man ahead of us in the trees; and, by the way he acts, I figger that he doesn't want to be seen by us. What do we do now?"

"Turn the wagon around," said Alston, "and give the mules the whip."

I stared up at him. He wasn't the sort of a man to give fool advice like that.

He corrected himself right away.

"No," said he, "there ain't room to turn it around. We've got to go ahead or stop."

"Stop," said I, "and they'll have a pretty good chance to bag the whole crew of you."

He nodded. His eyes were sparkling and snapping and his lower jaw was thrusting out.

"We can't turn around," said he. "If we stop, they eat us up. Could we break through them?"

"They're just beyond the top of the next hill," I told him. "We couldn't get any speed to drive us over the top of that rise. It don't look big, but it's enough to take all the roll out of our wheels. Besides, the ground is soft, over there; and the wheels will cut in too deep. You couldn't keep up a gallop—not with just these four mules!"

He nodded and swore. "That sounds like the fact," he admitted. "Then there's only one thing left. When the wagon gets down into the hollow, there, it may be that we'll be out of their sight; and, if we are, we got to try to slip out of the wagon and cut away through the trees. Is there much of a chance of that?"

I thought it over.

"One poor chance in ten," I told him.

"One change in ten is the best chance we have, then," said he. "Go get the girl back here into the wagon while I tie the arms of this Grenville."

58

AFOOT

HE KICKED ON THE BRAKES WITH HIS FOOT, SO THAT the wagon dragged down into the valley very slow and easy; and that gave us a few more seconds of time.

I ran back to Lou and told her to get down and skin for the wagon.

"What's up?" she asked me, as cool as you please.

"Gents with guns," said I, and waved ahead of me.

"Grenville, I suppose," said Lou, and jumped from the mule and ran back.

When we got there, we found that there was another obstacle that hadn't been planned on. Old William Daggett didn't understand, and there wasn't time to explain.

He said, "Gentlemen, gentlemen! If you wish to walk, by all means do so. But I am not very well, and I shall remain with the wagon. It is still some distance to my house, where I hope to make you fairly comfortable; but you will pardon me if I don't accompany you on foot."

"Poor old man!" said Lou at my ear. "He thinks he's taking us to his house to entertain us. Make Alston be gentle with him."

Alston said, "If I cannot persuade you, I'll have to—" And he reached for Mr Daggett's arm.

I pointed my finger at him like a gun. Well, it stopped him, but he was raving. "Curse you, what is it?" he barked at me.

"Easy with the old boy!" I told him.

"All right!" said Alston in a fury, jumping down to the ground. "Leave him behind—and leave all our hopes behind with him. I tell you, you fool, that we can do nothing without him."

"My dear sirs! My dear sirs!" old Daggett was saying, blinking at us. "What can it all be about?"

"You try, Lou," says I.

"There's robbers ahead of us, Mr Daggett!" she cries to him.

"Impossible!" says the old boy.

"Oh, we saw them!"

"In my valley?" says Daggett, very severe. "Well, well, I shall have to see to that. The rest of you have no fear. It is my pleasure to protect you—and fortunately I am armed."

With that he pulled out a little, old snub-nosed gat that must have been thirty years old, and he smiled down at it and then at us.

"You see you have nothing to fear," says he.

And there he sat, very tickled to be in at a fight, with the light beginning to glisten in his eyes, and a spot of color growing in his cheeks.

A very fine, noble-looking old fellow. He was the true grit, all right. It sure warmed my heart to watch him as he sat there with that gun shaking and wabbling about in his old hand.

"Of course you're not afraid, Mr Daggett," says Lou; "but we're all afraid. And I'm afraid! You'll come along to take care of me, won't you?"

"God bless me!" says old Daggett. "My dear child! Of course I'll come along and take care of you. Of course! Of course!"

The wagon had about got down to the foot of the slope as the old chap climbed down to the ground, and in an instant we were all of us in the brush.

The mules went on like nothing had happened at all. And the creaking of the wheels and the crushing of the sand and the gravel under the big iron tires made enough noise to cover the sounds that we made as we combed along through the trees.

We had enough encumbrances, though. There was old man Daggett, of course, still with his gun in his hand, telling everybody to hurry on ahead, while he would bring up the rear and take care that no harm overtook the rest of us. And he had to have Alston on one side of him and me on the other, to help him over the rough places and over the creek, because his legs were so stiff and weak and brittle with age and sickness. Then there was young Grenville. Alston was dead set on not letting him get away, and he kept Grenville in his eye all the time and was talking to him, too.

He said, 'Grenville, mind you, that when I shoot, I haven't got blank cartridges in the gun. You hear me talk? And I'll shoot to kill, as sure as you're a foot high."

For my part I believed him, and I could see that Grenville believed him too. There was nothing pretty about that Alston. He was mean and hard.

But that wasn't the worst. There was two big bundles, and those Alston insisted on taking along with us. I had to take one of them over my shoulder; and he took the other and waddled along with it, keeping one arm free for old Daggett.

You can see that we couldn't make any particular good time, being bothered and loaded down like this. And now, behind us and above us, we heard a yell of surprise and rage.

The wagon had been stopped, and it was known that we weren't in it. Of course that was the meaning, and there was a secondary meaning that interested us a good deal. By the volume of that roar we knew that there must be at least five or six in the party, and now they would scatter and try to find us.

Well, with five of us making tracks through the woods, how could they help but make a quick find and then come boiling up around us? I said that to Alston, and he nodded and gritted his teeth as he looked back over his shoulder.

"That's like that hound Grenville!" he snarled. "He knew just when the best time would be for hitting. We should have waited for night before we started to come into the valley."

"We would have been smashed up in no time," I told him, "if we tried to cover this road by the night. Besides, we're not beaten yet; but I think we'll have to fight before we're out of it. Is this why Grenville has been holding off? He's had men enough to eat up the party in the house."

"Of course! Of course!" snapped Alston. "What good would it have done him to grab the people at the house until this was there, too!" And he jerked his head toward poor old Daggett who was tottering along between us.

Finally we managed to cover a mile and a half, I should say; and there was no sound of any pursuit behind us. I knew that we would hear them a long time before we could see them. They would be sure to come on horses, and no horse in the world could wind his way silently through such a growth of brush and young sapling as grew through those woods.

We climbed up over the white ridge, where the big stones shoved their knees out of the ground. And then we could look straight ahead through the trees and see in the distance the form of the Daggett house, standing on the hill.

It had a great effect on old Daggett. He threw out his arms toward it, and then he staggered out and away from Alston and me.

"Let him go!" says Alston, frowning and watching very close. "He's got to get this out of his system some time."

"Ah, that is the place!"

That was all Daggett would say, over and over, "Ah, that is the place!" Not a happy tone, like a man seeing an old friend, but a wild, desperate sort of a voice.

"He remembers," says Alston. "The old goat remembers more than I suspected!"

We took hold of Daggett, one on either side of him. He gave us a wild look when we came up to him and grabbed him, and he made a faint struggle in our arms.

"Gentlemen," says he, "you have come for me, I see."

"We've come for you," says Alston.

"Ah, well, I did not think it would be so soon," said Daggett; "but there is truth in the saying that blood cries up from the ground, and that murder will out. Murder will out, no matter if it be buried seven leagues under the ground!"

He said it with a real agony in his throat, and I felt a wave of wonder and of fear. Because it didn't seem possible that this old fellow could ever have taken the life of another man.

"However," says Daggett, "I confess everything. There will be no need of a cross-questioning. And one of these trees will be quite as good as a scaffold for the hanging of my wretched body. But ah, may God forgive me! In my own house! In my own house!"

I looked at Alston. He was grinning with a sort of cold enjoyment, though the rest of us were all pretty sick. And I was almost glad when, right behind us, we heard horses smashing through the brush.

DANGER AGAIN

WELL, AS I WAS SAYING, THAT NOISE OF THE HORSES told us that trouble was coming and coming pretty fast. It broke up the concern with which we were watching poor old Daggett and listening to that talk of his that seemed to confess that he had been a murderer. With Grenville and his men smashing up behind us, I hardly knew what to think.

Alston said, "We got to put in among these rocks and try to stand them off."

He panted and pointed to a circle of rocks among the trees. But I could see in a minute the weakness of any scheme like that. The rock was all very well for gents on our own level. But what if Grenville and his tribe chose to slip up into the trees and fire down at us? They could butcher the lot of us as easy as if they had us herded into a pen.

But just what could be done looked hard to me to find out, when Lou run up beside me and lifted the bundle from my shoulder, where I was carrying it.

She jerked her head back. "You'll have to shoo them off, Doc," says she.

"Look here, Lou," says I, "are they a lot of flies, maybe, or deer, do you think?"

She just looked at me; and I knew my medicine; and I took it. I dropped back among the trees with old William Daggett making a terrible scene with Alston. He swore that he would die of shame if anybody but him turned back to face the danger. But they swung on through the trees and I saw no more of them while I looked back to see what sort of trouble would come my way.

Well, it came from two quarters. The gang of Grenville had been split into two sections. And those sections were driving up at us, one on either side of our trail.

The sun was down. I looked up between the great red trunks of the trees at the fire in the sky and the pure, deep blue of it up higher. There was a soft light everywhere, getting dimmer and dimmer; but it was enough light for shooting, and straight shooting, at that.

There were two things that might happen. I might turn loose some lead at the first riders I saw and turn them back, and that would give me a chance to slip away. Or else, when I started shooting, they might come right straight in. That would be the finish of me.

I got me a place not behind one of those whopping big trunks, but in a patch of brush in the center of an open space. From that spot I could see all around me pretty well, and there was enough brush to give me a sort of a screen, especially from men that were snap-shooting from the backs of horses.

I cuddled the butt of my rifle into the hollow of my shoulder and waited. And in another minute I heard horses crashing through the woods to the south of me— not far away, but just comfortably out of sight. I didn't like that. It meant that if I tackled the other lot, this southern mob would swing in and take me from the rear and scoop me up as easy as you please.

But straight before me came the other mischief. I heard some one shouting. I couldn't make out what, because the horses were making so much noise. Then three riders came in a bunch through the trees, with another pair behind them.

Of course by that time I was beginning to wish that I

65

could make back tracks, but it was too late. A lot too late, even if I wanted to lie still, because all five of them were driving straight at the spot where I was lying in the shrubbery.

Well, I began to pull the trigger of that repeater faster than I ever pulled a trigger before in my life, I know. I got a line just above their heads; and I fired three shots before they seemed to realize what was happening; and I fired three more while they made for the trees, all yelling:

"They're yonder in the brush! Scatter, boys!"

They got out of sight with a whoop, I can tell you; and I almost laughed. But I had no time to spend on laughing. My idea was to get their attention; and then, when they thought they had me at bay, to slip out on the far side of the shrubbery and so leave them there holding the bag, as you might say, with nothing at all in it.

But I needed speed if I was to succeed with that scheme. For I could hear the riders to the south of us shouting and coming on the wing to find out what was causing all the trouble. And all around me the trees were ringing with shouts and with the hoof strokes of the horses on rocks or through crackling brush as they tried to surround me.

I traveled like a snake and a little faster than most snakes, I think; until I got to the edge of the brush and saw before me, not more than six steps to the line of the woods, a flock of strong young saplings growing side by side like so many soldiers standing in a row.

But just as I raised up out of the brush, a rider came out of the trees from the south and with his revolver he put a pair of bullets not more than an inch past my nose. The smell of that lead, I might say, was all I wanted in the way of an argument to convince me that I should get

66

back to the brush as fast as possible.

There were two other riders behind the first man, and one of the two was that same Henry Grenville. They all had their guns out and they threw a pound or two of lead to comb the bushes where I was. One of the slugs stung my leg.

But there wasn't time to see what that wound was. Those three crazy men were driving right at me as though they wanted to ride on top of me, and I had to send a couple of bullets whirring that way before I could check them and send them piling back for the shelter of the trees.

Well, I had them at a distance from me, now. But here they were in a circle around me. And by the way they whooped and carried on, you would have thought they had their hands filled with a treasure. However, it was a bad mess. If they wanted to see me in the open, all they had to do was to touch a match to that brush and let the flames do the rest.

I waited to hear what would happen, and yet I got a small sort of satisfaction from the knowledge that the rest of the party was skimming along through the woods and making fast tracks for the house of Daggett on the hill. They might very well be where I was now, if I hadn't chosen to come back here and turn this trick.

And then it jumped into my mind with a stab of pain that the girl had sent me here. It hadn't been my own idea at all. It had been Lou's hunch. And how could I tell what had made her suggest it? Well, when I had taken that thought home in me, like a bullet, it made me postpone looking at the wound in my leg again. Because the hurt in my heart was a lot greater.

Maybe you have guessed how far the pretty face and the queer, careless way, and the strange eyes, and the husky voice of Lou had carried her with me. Well, I was wild about her. I had known her hardly an hour, and I was already lovesick for the first time.

It was the lowest time in my life, when I began to doubt Lou and her motives. I looked down at my leg, finally, and it wasn't much consolation to me to see that the bullet had only sliced along the surface of the flesh, just above the knee.

In the meantime a voice began calling, "Alston! Hello, Alston!"

It was the voice of Grenville. If he knew that Alston had been in the party, it showed that he was no fool. He had been taking it easy in the valley, waiting for Alston and his party to come. But from now on, Grenville would cut loose and do business. And things wouldn't be so very easy for the folks up there in the big house— not when they tried to get clear of Daggett Valley. No, that would be the time when they would wish they hadn't thrown me and my guns away!

HOSTAGES

I WAITED FOR ANOTHER MINUTE UNTIL GRENVILLE called again, "It's no use, Alston. We know we've got you. You might as well talk turkey to me now as later."

Then I sang out, "Hello, Grenville! Doc Willis, speaking."

"Hello, Willis!" he answered me. "I hear you, but you're not the person I want to talk to just now. Tell Alston that he had better talk for himself."

Another idea came popping into my head. By this time there had been plenty of minutes for Alston, Daggett, Grenville and Lou to get on to the Daggett

68

house. But if I could show Grenville that they were not with me, he and the rest of his men might pile away on the trail, hoping to catch up with the others. And then that would leave me free to break out.

Or, if only a part of them went, there would be less trouble for me to deal with the ones that were left.

So I said, 'Grenville, it's no good. You'll never talk to Alston here."

"He's deaf and cursing the world, I suppose," laughed Henry Grenville; "but that makes no difference to me. I could burn out the pack of you, if it weren't that you have the girl with you."

"You know that, too?" said I.

"Yes, I know about everything, Willis."

"There's one thing you don't know," said I. "And that is that Alston and Daggett and the girl are not here now."

"Not there now?"

"I came back here to hold you fellows for a while; and I think I've done it long enough, Grenville."

The minute I named the idea, they seemed to see the point of it. There was a general shout of rage and disappointment, and I could hear them making for their horses again. But then Grenville began to shout:

"Stay where you are! Stay where you are, everybody! We've missed the rest of them by this time. Do you think that Doc Willis would show the cards before their game was won? But I tell you it's not won for them, by a long shot, if we can get Willis into our hands! Let us land Willis, and we'll have the others pretty much when we please!"

That sounded very like sense to me. In the whole crowd, Zack and Roger Beckett were not much use at fighting. That left Alston and Buck Logan to bear the

69

brunt of the attack, and I didn't think they would have any very great luck in managing to hold off Grenville and his men.

However, here was Grenville sending his fellows back to their posts. The shadows were gathering pretty thick and fast.

He called, "Well, are you ready to come out, Willis?"

"What sort of a deal will you make with me?" I answered him.

He replied in a way that nearly took my breath. "You come with us, and I'll make you pretty good terms!"

Generous? Why, it was almost foolish. Here I was out of the picture, and all he had to do was to wait for his time to put a chunk of lead through me. But instead of that, he offered to take me on his crew as though I was a free man and had never done him a stroke of harm.

I said, "Will you let me come and talk with you on that?"

"Come out as free as you please," said Grenville.

"Show yourself first," said I. "Some of your gents ain't very friendly to me, and they might use the chance to shoot from behind."

"Here I am," says Grenville, and he stepped out into the open, as brave as ever he was. There was nothing of the yaller streak in that Grenville.

So I got up, in my turn, and walked out of the brush. I said, "I've come out here to talk to you, Grenville, because you're terribly white, it seems to me. But the first thing I got to say to you is that I can't go to work for you. I can't switch hosses in the middle of the stream."

"Is that final?"

"It is," says I.

"Well," said Grenville, "just tell me, if you please,

70

what you expect me to do with you?"

"You're the boss," said I, "I'd suggest something like this: They got your brother. And you got me. See if they won't arrange a trade for him?"

"They have Larry!" shouted Grenville.

"Why man," said I, "didn't you know that?"

He only groaned, "Is it true, Willis?"

"It's true."

"If they do him a harm," said Grenville, "I'll flay them alive."

Then he said, looking pretty sick and weak, "I never should have let him come. Think of a lad like that, blasting a fine life, with a sordid adventure—"

He broke off and snapped at me, "What happened?"

"About Larry?"

"Yes."

"He took a pot shot at me this morning, and my hoss Jupe got his head between the rifle and me. Jupe died, and I hit the ground alive. Afterward I got up behind Larry. Him and me had a little mix. And I persuaded him to come along with me, real friendly."

"Darn it, Willis!" said he. "You were born to ruin my plans. Is the boy hurt?"

"Not a scratch."

"And yet you had him under after he'd killed your horse?"

"That was it."

He rubbed his hard knuckles across his chin and stared at me. "All right, Doc," said he. "I'd like to turn you loose and let you go on your way for this; but before I can do that I've got to try my hand at getting my brother loose from Alston, and—Buck Logan."

He hesitated a little before he used that name, which made me suspect that he thought the opposition to the

71

scheme would come from Buck alone.

"You persuade Alston," said I; "and I'll swear that Buck will do what he can to get me back."

"Do you think so?" smiled Grenville. "Well, son, let me tell you this: They know that while they have my brother, they have a weapon that will keep me from bothering them a mite. If they can get the stuff they're after, they can walk right out of the valley with it; and I'll never be able to raise a hand at them, because they know that Larry means a lot more to me than all the money in the world. You understand? Now, Doc, you've had a chance to size up both Buck and Alston. Tell me frankly. Do you really think that either of them would prefer your safety to a fair chance to get away with the loot?"

I thought it over, and a lot of black thoughts swarmed up into my mind.

"About Alston I know," said I. "He'd never turn his hand to do me a good turn, or anybody else, except one."

"Meaning the girl," said Grenville.

"You seem pretty well informed," I couldn't help saying to him.

"Why, Willis," said he, "I know enough about that crew to be sick of them. But I could tell Alston, if I had the chance, that the girl is not for him. She has too much sense. He thinks he can buy her; but he can't—not in one short life!"

That pleased me a good deal.

"What do you know about her?" said I.

He squinted at me and then smiled. "Has she hit you, too?" said Grenville. "Well, she has a way about her, I admit. No doubt about that. But she's made quick work with you. Well, I know enough about her to respect her, if that's what you mean. But what you say about Buck Logan interests me a lot. Do you really think that he would put a high value on you, old-timer?"

"Do you think I'm wrong?" said I.

"You can see that I think that. But we'll see who's right in the long run. We'll not have far to run, at that. We'll go up there to the house and propose a dicker. A trade of you for my brother, and if Logan is the white man you think he is, he'll certainly see that the trade is made, rather than leave you in our hands. Isn't that right?"

I admitted that it was.

And so, in another five minutes I found myself sitting behind Grenville on his horse. He hadn't asked me to give my word that I wouldn't try to escape on the way. He didn't have to, because the rest of the gang were riding along behind us; and I would as soon have jumped into the fire as tried to get away under the guns of that lot.

I studied them in the evening light, and I'll tell you they were a hardy lot.

"Where did you get these thugs?" I asked Grenville.

"The finest lot of cutthroats out of jail," he chuckled; "but they'll serve their purpose. Here we are, old-timer. Now we'll see what happens with your friend in the Daggett house."

ENEMIES BARGAIN

WE CAME UPON THE HOUSE FROM BEHIND ONE OF THE nearest trees in the edge of the clearing that surrounded the old place. Grenville started shouting; and, in a few seconds, a window was thrown up by some one who took care to keep out of sight of us.

The voice of Buck Logan called out: "Hello, Grenville!'"

"It's Grenville," answered Henry Grenville. "I've come to talk business."

"Old son," said Buck, and his voice was that of a gent who is pretty well pleased with himself, "tell me what you got to say."

I've come to show you how generous I can be," said Grenville. "If you wish to listen!"

"Fire away."

"I have some property that belongs to your side of the fence," said Grenville.

"Have you?"

"You can guess what that property is."

"You mean Doc Willis, I suppose?"

"That's what I mean."

Buck Logan laughed; and, as the big sound of his laughter come floating out to me, it made me wince, I can tell you.

Grenville looked aside at me. "How does that sound to you?" he asked.

"Wait a minute," said I. "The party ain't over yet. We'll do the voting at the end of it."

"Just as you say. Listen!"

There was the big throat of Buck Logan bellowing:

"I hear what you have to say, Grenville. I never thought much of you as a business man, but I do now. You want to drive a bargain, do you?"

"That's what I'm here for."

"And you know that we have something that belongs to you, too? You know that, Grenville?"

"You have," admitted Grenville.

"Do you aim to say that the two parties should be

exchanged?"

"Why not?" said Grenville. "That kid brother of mine is no hand with a gun, and Willis is your fighting ace."

"You've told one lie," I said in an undertone. "That brother of yours shoots straight enough to satisfy me."

"I like the way you talk up," said Buck, "but I've got to say that you're looking at this thing pretty crooked, old-timer. I'd like nothing better than to make a friendly deal with you, but you got to look at it this way—so long as I have your brother, I've got you in my pocket. I'll have no trouble with you so long as I have him." And he broke out with his laughter again.

It brought a growl from Grenville. "Willis is thanking you for what you have to say," he cut in.

I could hear Buck Logan suddenly begin to swear in a deep rumble. "Is Willis there with you?" he asked.

"Willis is here," said Grenville.

"Hello, Doc," called Logan.

"Hello," said I, pretty feeble.

"Are you well, old man?"

"I'm well enough," said I.

"Mind you," said Buck. "Grenville is a white man; and I know that you're in no danger with him. Otherwise I'd cut off an arm to have you clean away from him."

I didn't make any answer. It was pretty thin talk, after what I had stood there and heard him saying just before.

"You there still, Doc?" called Buck, pretty anxious.

"Oh, I'm here," said I. "And I'm listening. Have you got any more to say?"

"Lots more! Lots more!" said Buck Logan. "And in the first place—"

"We've heard enough," said Grenville. "I brought Doc here mostly to let him see what a hound you are,

75

Logan; and, if I am not mistaken, I'll have him lined up against you before the morning!"

"Line him up! Line him up!" shouted Logan. "Line up a hundred more like him. Welcome to them, old-timer. But what I want you to notice is that I'll still have your brother Larry along with me; and while I have him, I'm not worrying, Grenville." He broke off, laughing again.

Grenville swore softly, under his breath. He called out, "I'm going off, Logan; but I expect you'll come to your senses after a time. You may think that I put a higher value on my brother than the case is; but you may be wrong—never forget that. And if you're wrong, with Doc Willis on my side, I can eat the rest of you alive, Logan! You hear me?"

"Good!" said Logan. "It'd be a fine meal. Especially considering what we'll have in our pockets before long. So long, old-timer! Keep a watch on this house; and, if I change my mind, I'll show you a pair of lights in this window."

"I hear you," said Grenville, "So long!"

He talked cool enough, but he was pretty sick at this sort of talk; and, as he went back through the trees, he hardly had the energy to tell a couple of his men to keep a watch over the house.

Then he walked on with me; and he said: "You've heard, Doc?"

"I heard," I admitted.

"And what do you think?"

"I'm not thinking!" said I.

"Come!" said he. "You have to confess that I was a good prophet. I told you what would happen, and what I said has turned out to be true. Is that right?"

I admitted that it was right, and I had to admit it with

76

a groan.

"I treated him white, Grenville," I explained, to let him know why I was so badly cut up.

"Of course you did—and you treat most people white, perhaps too white for your own good. If you had aimed to kill when we came up with you back there in the wood, perhaps you would be inside that house, yonder; and we would be burying our dead back in the clearing. However, let that go. I have two things to say. The first is the least important. It is that I still want you with me, and that I'll pay you five thousand dollars. The second is that I like you, my friend; and, if you play with me, you'll have a chance to see all of the cards laid upon the table face up."

"Right," said I. "I like what you say fine. And I dunno what it is that holds me back. It ain't that I care what people will say about me. I've had myself damned in about every known way, a long time before this. But, as a matter of fact, I don't think that I can go in with you, Grenville."

"You're sure?"

"I suppose I am."

"Will you give me one good reason?"

"I'll try to."

"You can't doubt that those fellows in there are all thugs."

"Daggett?" said I.

"Daggett?" said he, and his face and his voice softened a lot. "That poor old man! I'm sorry to know that he's in their hands, because he'll get no good out of it, whatever they may find in the house!"

"No good at all?"

"From those stone-hearted devils? I should say not!"

I shook my head. It was pretty hard talk, but I was

77

beginning to feel that Grenville was as right as the fellows in that house were wrong.

He went on, "What I want you to see for yourself is that if they will treat you badly now, they would plan to treat you badly even if you were with them, working heart and soul for them. Doesn't that stand to reason?"

I had to admit that there was a good deal in what he had to say; and he added, "Oh, I know them and I hate them as much as you'll come to hate them before you're done with them."

Then he made a pause and broke in, "Give me your answer, Doc."

I said: "I'd like to do it, but I started in this game with Logan and his crew inside of that house. They've never cut me off of their list. And I've got no more from them and this game than I might of expected from anybody that I was working for—unless he was my friend. And I think that I'll have to stick by them, Grenville."

"Ah, well," said he, "I'll change your mind for you before the morning. I've got to. Because if they have Larry, I've got to have something on my side of the fence to play off against that power—and what can it be except you? What can it be?"

Just then there was a call from the trees toward the house:

"Hey, chief, they've started in showing two lights from that window—"

I could hardly believe it, and Grenville shouted with his surprise; but, when we ran back through the woods and came to the spot, we saw that he had told us right. There was the two lights burning from the window where Logan said he would show them if he decided he must change his mind.

And they looked mighty good to me, I can tell you.

78

LOU DEMANDS FAIR PLAY

GRENVILLE SEEMED HARDLY ABLE TO BELIEVE HIS eyes. And he kept saying over and over, "I can't make it out. For Logan or Alston to do a thing like this! I can't make it out."

Well, for my part, I thought that when they had had a chance to consider everything, they had decided that it would be better not to leave me in the lurch; and so they had changed their minds.

There wasn't much of a dicker. Grenville just called out to make out what the meaning of the two lights in the window might be, and the answer came right back that it was what I wished for—Larry Grenville was to be turned over for me in a fair exchange. Out came Larry Grenville, walking straight down the path of the lamplight, and into the same path I walked freely toward the house. We met in the center, and Larry held out his hand.

"I thought I was done for in that fine gang of thugs, old-timer. I'm glad you were out there to make the exchange, but will you tell me one thing?"

"I'd like to if I can, Larry."

"How the devil did you ever hook up with such a low crowd?"

He didn't mean to be sassy. He was just speaking his mind out—and that was no great compliment to Alston, big Buck Logan, and the rest.

"They may look low to you," I told him, "and they may be low; but they're the crowd that I'm playing this game with, and they'll have to do for me." I could not help saying, "This here business is apt to turn into a fight, before long. And I give you one word of advice, keep clear of me, Larry, because you've used up your share of luck with me. But tell me one thing, what made them change their minds about making the exchange?"

"Can't you guess, you lucky dog?" asked Larry Grenville. "Why, it was the girl, of course. She just put down her foot and said she wouldn't take a step in the direction they wanted her to go until she saw you back in the house."

Take it all in all, I think that was about the best news I had ever heard.

"Thanks, Larry," said I. "I sure appreciate you telling me this."

He grinned at me in rather a crooked fashion. "It's all right, Doc," said he. "I was a loser with her before I ever had a chance to be a winner. So long."

He held out his hand. I took it with a good, hard grip, and then he passed on toward the woods, and I went on toward the Daggett house.

When I got to the door, there was Alston, opening it for me, and giving me a sort of a dark, sour, upward glance. He met me in silence; and I passed him and went on into the house, hating him with all my heart, I can tell you. Right back there in the hall I met Buck, and there was a good deal of difference. He came straight up to me and stretched out his big bear paw of a hand.

"Why, old-timer," said he, "dog-gone me if it ain't good to see you back here with us."

I looked Buck straight in the eye and tried to read something behind his big, ugly face. But all I could see there seemed like honesty, to me. Every time I came near him, lately, he had seemed more and more like a puzzle to me; and now I said:

"Look here, Buck. I stood out yonder under the trees and listened to the talk you made with Grenville. What

80

was I to make of that?"

"What were you to make of it?" said Buck. "Why, simply this—that I know Henry Grenville is a white man, and that you were in no danger with him."

"That sounds reasonable, Buck," said I; "but the fact is that while I was listening to you, it seemed to me that you didn't give a darn whether you ever seen me again. But beyond all that is the fact that while Grenville is a white man, right enough, he has a lot of thugs with him that hate my heart and that would plant me full of lead, if they had more than half a chance."

"Don't tell me that, Doc!" says Buck. "Don't tell me that, old boy!"

"You didn't know it?"

"Know it? Of course not!"

I stared at him, trying to make out whether he was joking, or whether he was really in earnest. He seemed in earnest, and there was nothing I could do to get at the real truth in him. If he wanted to deceive me, there was no doubt that he could do it. I was no match for that smooth-talking way that he had with him. He was altogether too deep for me.

I asked after Daggett, then; and Buck told me that Daggett had been in a terrible state by the time they got him to the house, and that he had been so nervous and cut up that they had put him to bed and quieted him down with an opium pill that Alston had.

"Old Daggett is pretty far spent," said Buck; "but he knew his house. He's pretty far gone; but, still, he knew his house. And that was one thing! However, I don't think he'll stay long in this here house. Not very long! And not long in this life, either, Doc, if I'm not mistaken."

I agreed with that. Because anybody with half an eye

81

could see that the poor old fellow was about two thirds dead.

Then I asked if I could see Lou Wilson.

He dropped his head a little and frowned, very thoughtful.

I snapped out, "Tell me straight. Are you afraid for me to see the girl?"

"No, I'm not afraid," said he.

But no matter what his words were, I knew that he meant something different. He was afraid. He was mighty afraid. Well, I could see him thinking the thing over, pretty careful, and then he said:

"Go ahead. You see Lou and talk with her. Only— you won't try to mix into her business and ours, too much?"

He looked at me with a frown, and I could see that he was on the edge of saying something more. But he checked himself and he only remarked, "Well, you go ahead and see her. She's upstairs. The first room on the right."

So I went up the stairs, thinking things over slowly; and, when I got to the first room on the right, I tapped at the door.

"Come in!" sang out the voice of Lou.

I opened the door and went in. And there was Lou standing in front of a mirror with her fine hair streaming down her back—but that hair which had been a fine brown during the day, was a bright, shining red at night!

THE PLOT BEGINS TO WORK

I DON'T MEAN THAT THAT WAS THE ONLY CHANGE. HER face was changed, too. There was a deep blue look about the eyes that had been gray in the daytime—gray and sky-blue, if you know what I mean. But here at night there was nothing about them except the deep violet blue that the eyes of beautiful women sometimes have.

I had never noticed her eyelashes particular before in the daytime; but now, though it was only the night, I could see them perfectly clear and fine, and that was a great surprise to me. They were jet black, and long.

But that wasn't all. No, even her skin had changed. It had been a fine, healthy-looking sort of a brownish skin before—an olive skin, if anything. But now it was very different, it was all pink and white. It was the sort of a skin that an eleven-year-old girl has before the sun has begun to roughen her up, and change her a lot, and make her wrinkled around the eyes. No, sir, she was so different that you wouldn't believe it; and that neck and throat of hers, that had been almost as brown as an Indian's, was now as snow and polished-up looking as a queen's might have been.

I was a good deal surprised, of course; and I hung there in the doorway and stared like a fool.

"Confound it!" says Lou; and she stamps on the floor. "Confound it, how was I to remember that you were back in the crowd again!"

I could see that she would not have cared if any of the others had popped in to see her, but I was different. I didn't know whether to be flattered or just sad.

I said, "Look here, Lou, what's wrong with you and your hair? Or are you Lou Wilson!'"

"I'm her twin sister," says Lou. "I'm the red-haired, blue-eyed kid; and don't you forget it!'"

Well, it was her voice. She might change the rest of herself, complete as a picture painted over; but she couldn't change that husky voice. It was Lou, right enough.

"What's happened?" says I.

"I tumbled in a stack of paints," says Lou; "that's all. Does it bother you a lot, old-timer?"

I couldn't speak, for a minute.

"Do I look like the devil?" says Lou.

"Nearly," says I.

She took up a mirror and squinted at herself.

"Why," says she, "the way it looks to me, I'm very nearly beautiful, in this rig."

Says I, "Lou, you take it from me. You was never meant to be beautiful."

She dropped the mirror and swung around at me. "Say, Doc, how do you get that way?" she snapped. "Am I as homely as all that?"

"I don't mean homely," said I; "but the fact is, Lou, that you—"

"Never mind," says she. "Don't explain. When I want to get the truth, I'll come to you. When I want to be happy, I'll go to somebody else."

Well, that was a good deal of a settler for me, as you can see for yourself; but at the same time, I wasn't finished.

"What's it all going to be about?" I asked her.

But just then a pair of voices floated up toward us through the open window and Lou didn't answer. It was old man Daggett, and Buck Logan was there walking along with him.

We heard Daggett saying, "In the morning I shall take you for a ride up and down the valley, as far as we can go."

"The whole length of it, Mr. Daggett?" says Buck, very respectful. "Will we have time for that in one

84

day?"

Daggett laughed a little. "You wouldn't think there was time, my friend Logan, looking at those trees. But let me tell you that the good road by which you come into the valley is continued up and down the entire length of it. I had it cut out; and I built the little bridges over every creek and gully, so that one can ride at a hot pace through the entire length and breadth of Daggett Valley—"

He added quickly, "Excuse me for giving it that name. But about a year ago, you understand, some of the miners who had struck it rich here, began to call the valley after my name; and it's become rather a habit here."

That took my breath, but I could see what had happened. Poor old Daggett had been snatched back to the old days, that long, long time ago, when Daggett Valley was still packed with miners, and when he had been the king of the place, looked up to, and worshipped, and respected a lot by everybody. Yes, he was back in those old days, and he was taking Buck Logan around and treating him like a guest, and trying to make him happy.

Somehow that gave me a sort of a tear in the eye, to hear Daggett talk like that. You could see in a flash just what sort of a fellow he had been in those old days, mighty generous, trying to make other folks happy, free and easy, proud of his fortune, and wanting to show it off to other folks.

"It'll be a fine trip," Buck Logan was saying. "It'll be fine to go with you, Mr. Daggett!"

"It will be my privilege—" said the old man; and then he stopped. For he had caught the sound of Lou's voice, she having exclaimed something about old man Daggett reliving the past.

"No," said old Daggett. "That was not my wife. Her voice is pitched high, and very light. It must be one of the servants."

"I been sort of wondering," says Buck Logan, "how Mrs. Daggett would get on out here in the wilderness, as you might call it."

"Ah! Ah!" says old Daggett. "Do you think it will be hard for a lady to be happy out here?"

"No, no," answered Buck. "That wasn't what I meant to say. Sure she could be happy here. Look at a fine, big house like this—why, any woman would be pretty proud and glad to live in it, I should say."

"I think so, too," said Daggett, pretty self-satisfied. "I think so, too! Why couldn't she be happy here? A little restless at first, perhaps! A little restless at first! But soon the beauty of the forest would begin to work on her mind—"

He was getting pretty excited.

"There ain't any doubt that you're right," said Buck Logan. "Besides," he added in a sort of a leading voice, "sometimes it's a good thing to get folks away from the city—a lot of bad things in the cities, bad for the men and bad for the women."

He said that with just a little weight on the last word, and I wondered that he dared to; but Daggett broke out with a groan, "Ah, Logan, that is true! That is bitterly true, of course! But here in the wilderness, a man can forget his past. And a woman can forget hers. Is not that true?"

"Nothing truer was ever said," remarked Buck Logan.

Well, that was enough explanation for the crazy thing that old Daggett had done in building this house away out here in the wilderness. It was something about his

86

wife—no freak of his own, but a thing that he had done for her sake. And I couldn't help pitying him more than ever, for he seemed almost tragic.

But I couldn't fit everything together. I couldn't make out the murder that he accused himself of. There were a thousand blanks in the true story that lived around the memory of the Daggett house. And, as I stood there in the night, I wondered how long it would be before I got at the truth. Or would I ever? I was a lot closer to the time than I guessed. And before the morning came I was to know everything that could be told of Daggett, and his poor wife, and Alston—yes, and of Carberry, too.

Well, just then the voice of Alston sang out, "Hello, Buck, are you there?"

"Here I am," says Buck.

"It's about time," says Alston.

"All right," says Buck.

"By Heaven!" gasped Daggett. "Whose voice is that?"

"Why do you ask?" said Buck.

"Because it sounded to me—no, it can't be—but it sounded to me like the voice of that archdevil, Alston!"

THE STAGE IS SET

WHAT A CHILL IT SENT THROUGH ME TO HEAR THAT! There was A man and a voice that Daggett had been traveling with for days and days, and suddenly he recognized it like a flash. But I suppose that being brought back to the old place had cleared up his brain. Not all of it—he was still a long distance from the normal. But he had recovered enough to have bright spots as well as the darkness; and so it was that he

87

recognized the voice of Alston—not out of the present, but out of the past of those long years ago.

There was electricity in the air, I can tell you. Right then I had the sense of a tragedy that was to come.

Buck took Daggett back into the house; and, as I watched him go, I wondered if the old man wasn't like a bull taken to the slaughter. I wondered if he'd ever come out again, alive.

After a minute, out came Buck; and I heard his voice calling softly, "Doc! Oh, Doc Willis!"

I looked at Lou, and she nodded her head for me to go.

I sneaked out, and then I waited until he called again. After that, I answered him; and I went out, because I didn't want him to think that maybe I had been overhearing what had been said between him and Daggett.

"You're here, eh?" said Buck.

"Yes."

"Have you seen old Daggett, lately?"

"No," said I. "Is he missing?"

"Not missing," said Buck; "but I wondered—well, let it go."

Of course he was hinting that perhaps I had overheard the conversation, but he thought that perhaps it wasn't important enough to emphasize.

He said, "There hasn't been a sound from the woods, eh?"

"No," said I, "there hasn't."

"Seems strange," said Buck Logan, "that Grenville should lie out there so quiet in spite of all the men he has with him. Don't it seem strange to you?"

"Yes," I admitted, "it sure does."

"What do you think he could have up his sleeve?"

"No idea in the world!"

He's planning some sort of trouble—some sort of real trouble for us," said Buck; "you can depend on that. He isn't the sort of fellow who would waste his time."

"I suppose not," said I.

"But you're keeping watch for us?" said Buck, quick and sharp.

"Am I the only one to keep up that job?" said I.

"Not the only one, of course," said Buck; "we're all keeping an eye peeled. But Zack and Roger Beckett, they ain't of much use, as you know; and me and Alston have Daggett on our hands."

"Sure," said I.

"Is there anything special up to-night?"

"Special? Tonight?" said Buck, and cleared his throat. "No, not tonight. The only reason I came out here was to tell you that we appreciate you, Doc. Also, I wanted to ask you to keep a sharp lookout now that we have the girl and Daggett here along with us."

"Sure," I said. "I understand. This here Grenville has been holding back and taking things easy, hoping that when the time comes he would be able to scoop up Daggett and the girl, either coming into the valley or after they got here. Ain't that right?"

"Exactly, Doc. Exactly."

"And now that the two of them are here, Grenville is going to cut loose pretty soon."

"Yes," said Buck, "and you never can tell when. A slippery devil, that chap Grenville is. Got a brain in his head that's working all the time, and you won't forget it."

"I won't forget it," I told Buck.

"And you'll stay busy on the job?"

"I will."

"I'll shake with you on that," said Buck.

Well, I took his hand in the dark, and then he started back towards the house. He strolled along; and he even whistled a note or two of a song; and then he went inside. By that time I was standing on a needle edge; for I was beginning to expect things to happen. There was a lot of reasons for what I expected to happen.

In the first place, there was no occasion why Buck should of made a point of looking me up there in the night except for a very definite purpose. And that was what he might want to make sure that he had got me outside of the house—important because of something that him and Alston wanted to do inside of it.

So I made up my mind to a number of things. I decided that right on this first night Alston and Logan were going to try to make their big play. And I decided, in addition to that, that they was going to try to make it right away.

But what was I to do? I couldn't guess what they would be about. I knew that it must have something to do with the make-up that the girl was wearing, but just what Lou was to be used for beat me complete.

Well, I looked over the house and I could see several windows lighted. One was the dining room. And one was the room of the old man Daggett, to the front of the house.

I turned the corner of the place; and there I seen another lighted window, one that opened out onto a little balcony, built strong and snug against the side of the house.

I decided right there that I would have to take a look, because I had to do something; and, guessing as much as I guessed, I would of gone plumb mad if I had had to stand around and look at the stars when robbery—

murder—I didn't know what all—might be taking place in the Daggett house.

The side of the house was pretty easy to climb on account of the big supports of the balcony that run down right to the ground. I climbed up, taking care not to make no sound at all, and I honestly think that nobody standing right under me could of heard a whisper from my work.

A good thing that I was so silent, too, because when I got to the outer edge of the balcony and lifted up, I seen that a man had reached the balcony ahead of me.

However, the important thing was not what was outside the window. It was what was inside the window. And that was about the queerest picture I had ever seen before—queerer, I'd make a guess, than you have ever seen, either.

There was a table right in the center of the space that I looked into through the window, and up to this table there was two chairs drawn. And in one chair sat Lou, but fixed up so you would never of knowed her.

Of course you can guess that she was made up the way I had seen her not a little while before, but that wasn't all. Her face was changed, then, but her clothes was changed now. She wore a big, broad, black hat, with a black feather curling down one side of it, and the brim looped up on the other side, like the pictures of riding hats you used to see in some of the old-fashioned books. And she had on a tailored suit; and around her neck there was a big brown fur, that looked like real fox, and mighty expensive. She had on a pair of black kid gloves, long and fancy looking; I mean to say that she had one of those gloves on, but the other glove was off and held in the covered hand. And the hand that was bare, why, it shone like anything. So that you wouldn't believe it! On one of the fingers of it there was a diamond that sparkled and glittered something wonderful to see. Yes, she had used up a considerable deal of whiting on those brown hands of her.

On the far side of the table from her there was a gent that I didn't know, at first. He wore longish black hair, and he had straight black-eyebrows that give him a sort of devilish look. And he was smooth shaven. He wore a black coat, padded out on the shoulders, the way coats used to be worn, a long time ago.

But in a minute this fellow smiled; and, by something in his smile, I knew him. Perhaps you've guessed already—yes, it was Alston! It was Alston, with his mean smile; but his gray beard was gone, which showed a good chin, and a straight, cruel, cunning mouth. He had covered up his gray hair with a longish black wig, with the hair of it brushed back a good deal, giving him a sort of an artistic look. And he wore a black silk cravat with a big diamond pin stuck into it—big enough and shining enough to stop a train with, I can tell you!

But I haven't told you all. I'll tell you that on the table between the two of them there was a smooth gray chamois bag, all crumpled up; and, spilled out of the mouth of the bag, there was a whole double handful of jewels.

By this time my slow brain was beginning to translate what I was seeing into the facts of the case. I knew, now, that this was a real effort to reproduce something that had been in this same room a long time before. But what could that be?

Pretty soon, Alston says, "Hush, Lou! What was that?"

"Somebody walking up the stairs," she answered him.

"Aye," said Alston, after listening for a moment. "But

92

is it time? No, not for ten minutes, according to what Carberry promised."

"Carberry?" gasped Lou, looking white even under her make-up.

"Why not Carberry?" said Alston. "He won't eat you."

"Carberry! The murderer!" says Lou.

"Darn it," said Alston, "I suppose I shouldn't of used that word. But I tell you, you'll never see Carberry's face—no matter how deep he may be in this thing."

"Ah," said Lou, with a quick glance over her shoulder toward the window; "I feel as if somebody was sneaking up behind me with a knife in his hand. Carberry!"

She was hard hit, and no wonder, considering the reputation Carberry wore around those parts of the world.

"Get ready!" said Alston. "Because I think they're surely coming!'"

"What'll I do?"

"Lean back in your chair; and, with your ungloved hand, grab at the jewels. You see?"

"Jewels?" said she, with a grin.

"Well, they look close enough to the real thing. I had this stuff made one at a time, to look like the real things; and I don't think I missed out, very far. He'll never know the difference unless he's seeing clearer than I think the poor old goat can do today. He's too upset to notice any of the details, I think. Lean back in your chair—so!"

She leaned back and grabbed at the jewels with one hand, just as he had said; and then Alston said, "I've got to lean over you now and pretend to be kissing you. You understand, Lou?"

"Did his wife do that?" said Lou.

"Why, she lost her head when she saw that there was a chance to get away from this place—worked out like a story. She spends all his money. Poor Daggett comes West to try to recoup. And he does, because he hits gold, with regular beginner's luck. After he's raked in a lot of the yellow stuff he thinks that he'll bring his wife West and keep her safely here away from all temptation to run up big bills and flirt with the boys. A wild man's notion! She would have gone mad in this place.

"And if it hadn't been for that, she would never have looked at—" He stopped himself.

"Never have looked as low as a gambler?" said Lou.

"Confound your sharp tongue!" says Alston. "No matter. The main thing was that he walked in and found us—Listen! They are coming toward this place!"

"Yes, right up the stairs—"

"And now down the hall! Hold this position, Lou; you hear me?"

He took her in his arms and put his face close to hers; and I think he would have made it more than just a pretense if she hadn't said, "If you really kiss me, Al, I'll sink a knife in you. You hear me?"

"You spitfire! You little devil!" he whispered through his teeth. "It would be almost worth it! Steady—don't tremble! That might give everything away. I'm the one who runs through the danger—not you!"

"Very well," said Lou. "I won't throw the game away, now that we've played it this far."

"Hush!"

I could hear the pair of feet stop outside the door—though they had been apparently trying to move very soft and easy. And in that minute I remember that my heart nearly stopped beating; and yet I had a chance to think of two things—the fierce, bright eyes of Lou, looking up to Alston, and the shadowy head of the gent outside the window.

Could that shadowy head be Carberry? I wondered. And then the door opened!

SEEN FROM THE BALCONY

OUTSIDE THE DOOR STOOD DAGGETT, LOOKING almost as small as a boy in comparison with the figure of the giant behind him. I thought that that shadow of a man behind must be Buck Logan; but just then he side-stepped back out of view, and I couldn't make sure. Daggett, I expected, would shout or make a start. But he didn't. He just walked into that room with a sort of a puzzled frown on his face, like a man who isn't quite sure of what he's seeing; and then he rubbed his knuckles across his forehead.

He leaned a hand against the wall. "Good God!" says Daggett. "This is what I saw in my dream!"

When he spoke, Alston jumped up and away, as though in surprise; and, as he jumped away, Lou leaned forward and covered her face with her hands, shuddering with real fear.

"Alston," said Daggett, "I knew I should find you here. Don't ask me how. God showed this thing to me, and I knew it must be!"

"God or the devil!" says Alston. "Stand away from that door, Daggett; or I'll do you harm."

"Are you running away?" says Daggett. "And are you leaving your woman behind you?"

Lou gave a twist and a sort of a moan. Alston backed into a corner of the room, with his right hand always

95

behind him and in his hip pocket. I never saw a man do any better acting.

"Daggett," says he, "you're wrong. She's not mine. Only—just now—"

"Just now you planned to run away with this? Is that all? And she is wearing a hat—by accident, I suppose?"

He stepped to the side and looked at her. "And a riding skirt, too!" said he.

"Curse it, man," said Alston, "I want to explain—"

"Hush!" says Daggett, very grand. "Hush, Alston! Don't you suppose I understand perfectly? I understand everything. And the reason you wanted me to put more and more money into jewels, Martha, I understand that, too. There's only one thing that rather bothers me—not more than a third of those fine fellows are mine! And where did you get the others? Where did you get the others, Alston—or should I ask that question of you, my dear wife?"

You could see that he was holding himself back with a hand of iron, but all the time I kept waiting for that iron hand to snap.

Alston glared at Daggett, and then at Lou; but Lou did not stir. And Daggett picked up a big ruby—a monster and a sparkler.

"Here's a beauty," said he, "that must have cost a good many tens of thousands. I know a bit about the prices of rubies, now; and I wonder how much this thing cost. More than a hundred thousand, I should say. A hundred thousand in one sparkler! Ah, Martha, you and Alston truly have high stakes on the table! Very high! Very high!"

He looked across at Alston and tried to smile, but it was a terrible poor excuse for a smile that he worked up.

"More of them, too," says he, "a great many more!

96

Why, Martha, you've let yourself in for your share of a very tidy fortune, here. A great deal more than I could offer you at present, it seems! A great deal more!"

His smooth voice wobbled a bit, here; and his hand went up to his wrinkled old throat.

He went on, "I see no good reason why I should not take these jewels and the rest, which belong to me, and try to ascertain if they may not have been stolen—as mine were about to be. Do you think of any good reason to advance against this, Alston?" And he scooped the stuff all together and raked it into the chamois bag.

"Will you look at me, Martha?" said he. "Poor girl, are you really going to give up everything and go off with a rascally gambler like Alston? Alston of all the men in the world! How will you be considered in the East, after this is known? You should know—because that world means a great deal more to you than it could ever mean to me."

He put the chamois bag into his pocket; and, as he did that, Alston barked at him, "Daggett, drop that bag on the table, do you hear me? Put it back where you found it!"

"You speak harshly," said Daggett, looking more at his 'wife' than at Alston.

"I mean business," said Alston. "Your own stuff you may take out, but the rest has no concern of yours attached to it!"

"How can I be sure of that?" said Daggett, gravely. "I tell you that the property of every honest man is the concern of every other honest man. And how can I tell that these sparklers really belong to you—and to Martha?"

"No other person has claimed them," said Alston.

"I claim them, then," said Daggett, "until the law

97

decides otherwise!"

"Daggett!" barked Alston, raising his voice sharp and hard."

"Don't do it!" said Daggett, shaking his head in a sort of a sad fashion. "Don't bring out your gun, Alston. I warn you that this evening I am armed. And the truth of what will happen here is revealed to me—I cannot say by what marvelous foresight. But if you draw your weapon I shall shoot you through the head and leave you dead on this floor—stretched beside the table, there. I have seen it all in a vision, Alston, and the very manner of your fall. I beg you in the name of Heaven, believe what I am telling you. You have planned too much harm against me already, and you are given into my hands now. Will you believe me, Alston?"

Alston, backed into the farthest corner of the room, swayed a little from side to side; and it was wonderful to see the way he made fear and shame and a pretended desire for those faked jewels fight in his face. But finally he said:

"Well, let it go. I only want you to realize, Daggett, that you are changing parts with me, and becoming the real robber where I was only trying to be a robber. And what the law will say to you—"

"I shall be very willing to meet the law face to face," said Daggett, "quite as willing—or perhaps a little more so—than you can be. But—"

He broke off, "I have warned you, Alston. Beware of me!"

"Curse you and your warnings!" said Alston. "And take this!"

He snatched out a revolver and fired, and I saw Daggett swing his old head to the side and drag out the old revolver that I had seen before. While he swung it up, there was time for a handy man like Alston to of fired again half a dozen times. I was about to break through and stop the slaughter, when all at once I remembered that this was only an acted scene—acted by everybody except old Daggett. He was in the deadest sort of earnest. He brought his old gun down on the mark and fired.

Alston let his Colt drop with a clatter to the floor, and he clasped his hands over his head and staggered forward. He pitched on his face beside the table and twisted over on his back and lay still in a sprawling shape, with a great smear of red down his face and through his hair; and in his hand I could see the little red sponge with which he'd done the trick—in or under his hand, away from the view of Daggett.

As for Daggett, he stood up stiff and straight for a minute, and then dropped the gun into his coat pocket.

"I knew it would happen exactly like this," he said quietly. "I knew it with a very strange fore-knowledge. Martha, God have pity on your wretched soul, because you were the cause of this. You were the cause of this—"

All at once there was a heavy knocking at the front of the house. It made my hair stand on end, and it seemed to throw a terrible chill into Daggett. He had been as calm as could be, up to this point; but now he went off the handle in a wild way, throwing his hands above his head. He turned into a child, very pitiful to see.

"Martha! Martha!" says he. "What shall I do? Oh, what shall I do? Help me, Martha, in Heaven's name! Help me, I pray you!"

She only flung herself out of her chair, without giving a chance to see her face, and kneeled beside Alston.

And I could see Alston's lips move as he said, "Good, girl! Well done! Well done!"'

"You treacherous devil!" groaned Daggett. "The whole world is against me, and I have killed a man—"

He turned and plunged from the room just as the knock in the front part of the house was repeated. At the same time, the shadowy shape of a man which had been kneeling in front of the window jumped up and turned around toward me with a grunt of excitement; and I gave him something that I had prepared for him a long time before—the long barrel of my Colt slammed along the side of his head so that I thought that I could feel the skull spring and bend under the shock. He gave one gasp and flopped on his face on the floor of the balcony, just as old Alston, within the room, scrambled to his feet and started to say, "Honey, you worked it like a fine actress. And now if Carberry—"

Here he heard the gasp from the balcony and turned his head sharply toward us.

"What's that?" he snarled. "Go and see, Lou. Because if—"

I didn't wait to hear any more. I dropped from my place and shinnied down the pillar and dropped to the ground; and, as I jumped away, a gun spurted fire above me, and a bullet almost tagged my head. It was Alston, standing on the balcony and raging like a madman, because I suppose he saw now that this fine scheme of his, the deepest and the smartest that ever any crook ever invented, was now wasted and all gone to pot.

However, I didn't have any chance to stand there and think these things out. I just ducked around the corner of the house and out of range of that barking gun of his; and, as I ran, I jerked out my own Colt again. A right good thing I did, too!

THE HIDING PLACE

ALL THE DEVIL HAD BROKE LOOSE AROUND THAT house, I can tell you. I heard some one shouting, off in the woods; and then there was the sudden roaring of a pair of guns in the basement of the house; and then the scream of a man in a terrible lot of agony. Dying, I supposed—because the scream ended quick and short and sharp.

I ran straight on, beginning to wish that I was well out of this mess, and wondering how long it would be before Grenville and his gang jumped that house and scooped up everybody that was in it. And just as I got that idea I see a door open in the bottom of the house where I had never knowed that there had been a door before. I seen that door opened, and a man run out into the trees.

Sort of by instinct, I yanked up my gun to be ready for trouble; but this gent he run straight past me, and I seen that it was old Daggett. He had his gun in one hand, and he had the chamois bag in the other; and, though he passed within a few feet of me, he didn't seem to guess that I was there.

He ducked into the trees; but, after he had gone a step or two he stooped, and he jerked up what looked to me like a stone that weighed half a ton. He jerked that stone up and throwed the bag in under it, and then he turned around and he run back to the house and entered in through the side door. And that door closed after him, and there was the side of the house looking just as it had looked before.

The noise had all died down, too. I felt almost as though I had been dreaming these things, and had

101

waked up like a sleepwalker.

The first thing I did was to run to that big-looking stone and lay hold of it. No, it was only a surface slab; and it come up light and easy in my hand. I picked out the chamois bag; but when I did that, my hand touched something else in there. I lighted a match and looked.

It was the rotted shred of something that looked as though it might of been chamois in its day. But it was rotted by dampness and time; and its contents was spilled out onto the gravel; and I seen that there was a collection of jewels like them that had been on the table in the room upstairs just a little time before.

Well, it let in light on my slow head, at last. I seen the thing in one great crash.

In those old days, Alston had come to this house carrying with him loot that he got by stealing or by gambling. You couldn't hardly tell which. And he had aimed to collect pretty Martha Daggett—just as he had aimed to collect Lou Wilson, this next time. And he had been about to walk away with the girl and the jewels when in steps old Daggett—who maybe had come back early from a journey; and Daggett had spoiled everything. He had shot down Alston, and he had run down through the house.

Nobody knew where he had gone. They took it for granted that he had hidden the loot in the lower part of the old house, and that was the reason they had searched and searched. But why they hadn't simply torn the house to bits in the search was because this treasure was such a dog-gone small handful that nobody could very well hope to find it if the house was turned into debris.

So, finally, the grand scheme had come into the head of Alston when he seen, in Denver, a girl that had the same sort of features that Martha Daggett had.

He had come out here; and he had staged this thing, fixing up the house and getting it all ready so that it would look just the way the place had looked in the old days—or near enough to the way that it had looked to fool a half-witted old man. And then everything was rehearsed just the way it had turned out on that other night—except that this time there was to be a close watch on where Daggett ran, and what he did with the sparklers.

And that was where this here fine scheme had broken down. Perhaps that scream that I had heard in the house explained a part of it. But anyway, the gent or the gents that was to watch where Daggett run had lost out. And only by chance I had come onto the spot where the old man put the loot.

I thought this out in half a dozen seconds, while I was taking up the jewels. And then, as I cupped them in my hand, I wondered who there was in the world that would take them away from me—excepting the part of them that belonged to Daggett, and which I swore should go back into his hands and to nobody else's.

There was other parts of the whole thing that I didn't understand at all. And among the rest of it, I couldn't make out just where Buck Logan fitted in, because he was certainly more than a mere overseer of the work on the house. Neither could I tell where Carberry belonged; and I half suspected that I would never know, because Alston had promised the girl that she would never see the face of the old bandit. Then there was the Grenvilles. How did they come into the picture?

Well, time would take care of all of that, I thought. Then I decided that the first thing I should have to do was to go find Daggett. I wanted to get Lou out of this mess; but I felt somehow that no matter what happened,

103

Lou would be pretty well able to take care of herself. Old Daggett, he was a different matter.

How he had managed to get clear of the house in spite of the rest of them, I couldn't tell. It was beyond me how he had been able to fool old Alston and such a sharp fellow as Buck Logan; but the fact was that nobody had seen him leave the house, and maybe no one had seen him enter it again.

Now, maybe I was wrong, after all; for just as I was about to start toward the house, I saw the same section of the bottom of the wall swing open like a door, and three men came sneaking out. They came slowly up toward the woods, playing a strong light over the ground.

"This is the way he came. No doubt about that. I could swear to these footsteps!" said a voice that I thought I knew.

A moment later, as they came closer, I heard him say again, "Here he went, running all the way. Who would have thought there was such life in the old chap?"

I recognized the voice for certain this time. It was Henry Grenville.

"Then how come that he turned around and went back into the house?" one of the other two asked.

"Maybe we'll find that out in turn," said Henry Grenville. "The first thing is to run down these tracks."

"What a mess Logan is, eh?" said another of the three. "Never seen a face like his!"

"And he hollered loud enough!" says another.

"He had reason, poor devil," said Grenville. "He had very good reason. I don't think he'll ever see the light of day again. He's paid for his part in this game!"

"Blind forever!'"

"Yes, I had a good look at his eyes. They're ruined."

104

That was a shock for me, but hardly as much as the next thing I heard.

"Maybe he deserves what he got," says one of Grenville's helpers. And Grenville himself answered up quick and sharp, "Deserves what he got? That devil deserved to be burned alive, inch by inch! There never was such a scoundrel since the world began. Even that Alston is a white man—almost a saint, compared with—Logan!"

Well, I have traveled with Buck, bunked with him, cooked for him, eaten with him, and pretty near done everything except fight with him; and I couldn't see why he come in for any such talk as this, which was pretty sweeping, as you got to admit. But there was no doubt that there must of been something in what Grenville said, because he wasn't the sort of a man to say things rash. He was a man who would have reasons for what he said, and that had a lot of weight with me.

Well, I watched the three of them follow up that trail, talking softly to each other, all the way, until they come to the spot where the big, flat-topped rock was.

"Here the trail ends—try that rock," said Grenville.

Then, in a minute I heard a deep chorus of voices, partly discouraged and partly excited; and I knew that they had found the place and they understood what it meant.

"Here's one stone—one diamond!" said Grenville presently. "Some fox has been here before us. Now, let's find the man!"

POOR OLD DAGGETT!

WELL, I COULD HAVE CURSED MYSELF PROPERLY TO think that I had waited there until Grenville and his men

105

came to that conclusion. If I jumped up and started running now, they would be sure to spot me; and, though it was a dark night, they had a spotlight to show them where to shoot.

"This way!" I heard Grenville saying. "See how short his steps were! He was lighting matches, here, and looking at the loot."

By this time I was working my way out of that clump of brush which had looked so good to me and so safe to me a little time before. I got into the clear, but it took me a terrible lot of time, for I had to feel my way along in the pitch dark, and treat every limb of the bush as though it were a bottle of nitro-glycerine.

But clear I was, at the last—and I got up on my hands and knees and sneaked off a little ways until I thought it might be safe to stand on my two feet.

Just as I was about to sneak off at a run for the corner of the house, there was a sudden flash of light that fell across me from their spotlight.

"Mind your footing!" snapped Grenville.

But one of the others called in an excited voice, "Did you see that? Who was that?"

"Where?"

"There! There he goes!"

I was up and away; but, as I jumped into full speed, their light steadied and shot full at me.

I dodged out of the path of it as I heard Grenville sing out, "Willis! It's Willis! I might have guessed he would be on the inside when the crash came. Boys, if you down him, we are rich!"

They found me with that flickering light again, and three guns smashed at the same time. I felt a bullet knife through the upper part of my left arm; and then I turned the corner of that house a little faster than a running deer when the hounds give tongue behind it. They followed as fast as they could; but they would have needed wings to get me, after that.

I had intended to cut off toward the woods. But by the hot spurt of the blood down my side, I knew that I needed help, and that I needed it quick and bad.

I rounded to the front of the place, leaped up onto the porch, and kicked open the front door.

I slammed it behind me in time to have it splintered from top to bottom by two or three bullets. And at the same time I heard two voices shouting in the bottom part of the house; and then two guns sounded in quick exchange.

After that there was silence again. No one seemed to be stirring on the outside of the place. And on the inside there was a terrible dead silence for another moment— then I heard a faint groaning from the bottom part of the house.

Well, I glanced down to that arm of mine and I knew that I would have to find a friend and find one quick. So I put my head back and shouted, "Lou! Lou Wilson! D'you hear?"

I waited another minute. A door slammed somewhere.

Then, "Hello! Doc?"

That was the voice of Lou, and nothing ever sounded half so good to me as her voice when she was singing out. I went up the stairs three at a time; and I found her on the landing above. She grabbed me.

"What's happened? What has happened?" she gasped.

"I don't know half," said I, "but just now the main thing is for you to leave go of my left arm. It's been hurt and I want you to tie it up for me."

"Here's the hospital," said Lou. "Come in with me!"

107

She took me into the same room where she had been sitting with Alston when things began to happen. Alston wasn't there now. But young Grenville sat in a chair in one corner of the room, slumped far back, his eyes closed, and a bandage tied around his head and passing over a part of his face. I didn't have to ask how he had got that. It was where the long, cold, heavy barrel of the Colt had landed when I knocked down the man who had been with me on the balcony outside of the window.

But Larry Grenville wasn't alone there. Lou was right in calling it the hospital. At the table there was a big hulk of a man sitting with his face in his arms, and his arms resting on the table. By the wide look of his shoulders I knew that it was Buck Logan. He raised his head. There was a bandage right straight across his eyes, and I guessed that Harry Grenville had been right when he said that Buck was blinded.

"What happened, Buck?" said I.

"Plenty," said he, as cool as you please. "How are things with you, kid? You'll have to tell me. I'm through with seeing for myself."

"It's not as bad as that," I told him. "It sure can't be as—"

There was a little cry from Lou, here; because she had got my sleeve cut away and she was seeing the wound and the blood that was welling out of it. But she didn't make any fuss; she went right on like a brave girl, and begun to tidy up that wound, and then to put a dressing on it.

"It's as bad as all that, though," replied Buck. "I'm a gone goose, kid."

"What happened?"

"I was down in the cellar, waiting till Alston had scared old Daggett that way. And when he came, like a

108

fool I let him see me. I forgot that he had a gun with him."

"A gun loaded with blanks," said I. I remembered the sound of the shot that Daggett had fired at Alston when that crook pretended to fall dead under it.

"Loaded with blanks, yes," said Buck. "But when a blank is fired close enough, what happens? Think of a cat spitting fire!"

Well, that was enough to tell me what I wanted to know. You watch the spurt of a Colt fired in the night and you know what I mean. The jump of the fire goes quite a little distance, and I knew that the burning grains of powder had spurted into the eyes of Buck Logan. I remembered, too, that the scream that I had heard from the bottom part of the house not long before old Daggett had come running out. And that was it! It was the yell of Buck when that torment was shot into his face. Enough to break even his nerve, though that was stronger than good-proved steel.

Well, I had had a good many doubts about Buck, but when I seen him sitting there so quiet and so calm, I had to put a hand on his shoulder and say, "Buck, old-timer, I'm sure sorry! I'm mighty sorry! But the doctors these days can fix up pretty near anything; and they'll fix up you, too! Wait and see, you'll be all right."

He smiled. Have you ever seen a man smile when his eyes was covered? Leastwise, with Buck, it was like watching the grin of a wolf."

"I've got what's coming to me," says Buck. "I don't whine. I'm finished. But when you get your arm tied up will you do one last thing for me, Doc?"

"Sure," said I.

"Thanks. It'll be about the last thing that I got to ask from anybody, I suppose. But go down and find Alston.

He'll be around in the lower part of the house, messing about. Get Alston and bring him back up here. But don't say that it's me that wants him. I got to have a talk with him. you hear?"

"Sure," said I, "and I'm fixed up fine right now!"

I got downstairs; and I turned to the cellar door, and through it I soft-footed for the cellar beneath, because there was where I was most likely to find Alston, according to what Buck had said. There I found him, too, being led to him by a faint glow of a lantern.

He was too busy with his work to pay any attention to me. He was working away at the wall, taking out stone after stone as quick as he could free it from the cement. And already he had cleared away enough to show a great gaping hole—a hole that led not outside into the night, but into a vacancy between the two walls that had been built there. It looked pretty ghostly; but I could remember how old Daggett had seemed to walk out of the solid side of the house, and I could guess what Alston was after.

And Daggett? I thought he was asleep, at first, for he lay on his back, stretched out so peaceful with his eyes closed. But then I seen the purple splotch at the side of his head, and something about the stillness and the stiffness was enough to make me understand—even though I hadn't stopped to think that he wouldn't be lying down here asleep on the cold cellar floor.

No, he wasn't sleeping. He was dead. I remembered the two shots and the groan. Alston must have done the rotten thing, though I couldn't see how even Alston could ever get as low-down as to do a murder like that one.

I slipped up behind him and put the cold mouth of my Colt against his neck. He sagged forward and drew in

110

his breath with a bubbling sound.

"Get up, you coyote!" says I.

He waited half a second.

"Willis!" said he.

"Maybe!" says I.

"Curse the day that ever made Logan hire you!" says he. "What do you want with—"

Don't turn around, and put your hands up good and high. I sure like to see them that way—as though you was holding up the roof from falling. That's just the way I like to see you, old-timer."

"All right," says he. "But why all the fuss?"

"I don't know," says I. "I was sent for you!"

"Did Logan send you?" he asked quick and sharp.

"No," I lied. "You've asked enough questions, and now I'll ask a couple. What happened to old Daggett?"

He didn't even bother trying to deny it.

"Silly old fool was stubborn. He irritated me too much. Where do you want me to go?"

"March ahead of me," said I, "with your hands up all the way. Poor old Daggett! I tell you, Alston, I'm aching and yearning and longing to kill you. I hope you'll give me a fair excuse. And I'll tell you this— you're the first man I've ever met that I'd as soon shoot through the back as through the face. You hear me talk?"

He heard me, and a little wriggle ran down his back as the chilly idea that I was all in earnest went to his black heart. Then he marched on ahead of me without a word.

I herded him up the stairs. And only when he come to the door of the room where the rest was, his eyes turned toward Logan, and he hesitated a little.

"Good!" said Logan.

111

But I looked chiefly at the girl, and her face was a study of disgust and contempt as she eyed Alston.

"Not even dangerous—to a man!" said she.

"Here he is, Buck," said I. "And now, old boy, what do you want with him? He's got his hands up in the air."

"Oh, none of that! None of that!" says Buck. "Him and me are friends for too long to need anything like that. I want him to sit down here close to me. That's all. Set him down in a chair close to me."

I told Alston to do what was ordered; and, when he sat down, Buck put out a big brown hand and gathered in one of the wrists of Alston. And I seen a shudder go through Alston's body. He was a pretty sick-looking fellow, if ever I seen one."

"Gents," said I, "I dunno what's in the air here; but I got to tell you this. Here is Alston, the only uncrippled gent that we got left; and Grenville and his bunch are all outside and raving and tearing to get inside this here house because they know that the jewels of Daggett are here."

"How do they know that? How do they know that?" snapped Alston.

"How do we know that they're here?" I asked, sneering.

"Forget about the jewels, Al," said Buck. "Hear me chatter, will you?"

GUN PLAY

"WELL," SAYS BUCK, "I'LL ONLY KEEP THE ATTENTION of you gents for a few minutes. I want to tell you about a couple of boys. One was a bad boy that used to punch the noses of the other boys in the school. And one was a

112

good boy that was always at the head of his class and that was so smart that he knew how to have his fun and always shift the blame of it onto the head of the bad boy. And yet when there come a pinch, he always knowed how to make the bad boy his friend, and to use him.

"Buck—" says Alston, getting white.

"Never mind, old-timer!" says Buck. And he begins to pat and stroke the hand that he was holding. I felt that something pretty dreadful was in the offing, but I couldn't guess what.

"Well," says Buck, "the bad boy left the school. Run away—and he didn't go back no more. But a long spell later on, when he was a young buckaroo, he meets up with the good boy. Says the good boy, "There is lots of gold in the camps, kid. I'll go inside and work them with the cards. You stay on the outside and work them with your gang. I'll feed you the information that you need all the time. And you and me will split up the profits, understand?"

"Well, the bad boy thought that this was pretty good. He done the thing. The good boy played cards and got the information, and he passed it out to the bad boy; and the bad boy, he got into the swing of holding up gold shipments and having a good time all around. And being bad, he had fights. And being a steady hand, when he had a fight, he most generally did a little killing. You understand?"

Oh, I understood, well enough. We were hearing the inside history of Alston and somebody else—and the name of Carberry was the one that was behind my teeth. I would of given a lot of money to know how Buck come to hear all of this stuff.

"Finally they made a big pot," went on Buck.

113

" 'What are we gonna do with this stuff?' " says the bad boy.

" 'Turn it into jewels. They bulk down even smaller than bank notes,' says the good boy, who had a pretty wise head on his shoulders."

"So they each turned their half into jewels, and they met up and counted over the shiners what they had collected and admired each other and the size of the pile that they had got together.

"The bad boy, he proposed a drink. And the good boy said that it was a darned good idea, and first he slipped a little pinch of knock-out drops into the booze of the bad boy.

"And after the bad boy had taken the drink, he gave a yawn and went to sleep.

"The good boy took all of the loot and disappeared. And the bad boy, he pretty near died from the effects of that stuff, because the good boy had meant to kill him with the poison; and nothing saved the bad boy from dying except getting powerful sick.

"Well, when the bad boy got his senses and his health back, he says to himself that he has been bad for a long time, and killed his men and done a lot of damage; and here he winds up in the end with a good chance of getting himself hanged, should the news of him ever leak out. But he decided that he would now try his hand at going straight. So he got himself a new name and a string of mules and started being honest. And he thanked Heaven that his face wasn't known, tied to the name of Carberry!"

The cat was out of the bag, now.

Alston gave a gasp and he says, "You idiot, Buck—what do you mean?" And he reached back to his hip pocket.

"Steady, Alston!" says I. "Remember what I told you while we was coming up the stairs!"

And I tilted my gun down and watched him through the sights—not a pretty picture, either.

Buck went drawling on, "But after I had gone straight for a long time and begun to respect myself and the rest of the world, pretty much, along comes Alston and says to me, "Carberry, this is the time for us to make a grand clean-up. Point your gun the other way. It won't do you any good to kill me now because I tried to kill you and did rob you that other time. The thing for you to know is that the stuff I stole from you I lost afterward. And more besides! Your stuff, Carberry, and mine; and the Grenville jewels that I lifted and had along with me; and the gems I polished off a chap by name of Daggett! This here Daggett was about to lose his stuff through his wife—when he popped up, shot me down, and then went mad and lost the stuff where he himself couldn't find it. But I have the world's greatest scheme for making Daggett himself lead us to that loot. And a grand big fortune it is!"

Alston put in with a sort of a scream, "He lies! He lies like the very devil!"

"But in this deal," said Buck Logan, alias Carberry, "I've collected my finish. And now, Alston, you've come to your finish, too!" And as he said that he yanked at his clothes and brought out a Colt that looked about a yard long to me and black as a bucket of paint.

Alston screamed like a wild man and jumped up and snatched out his own weapon. He fired first, and Buck sank onto his knees, a dying man; but he still had hold of Alston's hand, though Alston was screaming and fighting to get away. And Buck dragged him closer and reached out his Colt until the muzzle of it got to the

115

body of Alston.

Then he fired twice.

I got to him in time to knock up his hand after the second shot; but I was a long, long time too late. Alston dropped dead; and Buck sagged down on the floor, his big head wagging from side to side.

I forgot everything except the jolly old days when we'd followed the mules up the trail toward the valley. I forgot all the lies and the double crossing.

"Buck!" said I.

"Is he dead?" says Buck.

"Yes," says I, "and for the killing of him you pretty near deserve a reward, Buck!"

"The reward I deserve is what I'll get!" says he. "Shake hands with me, kid. And remember this here one thing, will you—that the white man you knowed by the name of Buck Logan was white, though his name wasn't Logan, and—"

He died there, and I felt the strength go out of his big hand. But I couldn't see his dead face. There was too many tears in my eyes.

Which would prove that even a Carberry could be loved by a friend; but nobody on God's earth would ever dream of grieving for half a minute for that rat Alston. Or for any of his kind!

Now that Buck is finished, there don't seem much energy in me for telling the rest. Because, really, the rest was all happiness.

Before we left that house we had to make a dicker with the gang of Grenville—I mean that Lou and me did—that we would let the first sheriff be the umpire. The first sheriff was. He come and seen the house and he heard the story. He took the loot and groaned.

116

"Why wasn't I born to be a crook?" says he. And then he turned around and put me in jail!

Well, that was just his way of seeing that I got justice; and I sure had plenty of it before I got through. For five months they seesawed up and down, until they finally got it clear in their heads that I hadn't killed nobody.

By that time Lou and me was only waiting to get married. And by that time the jewels had been gone over. Larry and Henry Grenville were able to pick out the stuff that had belonged in their family. And other folks turned up here and there to make their claims. Yes, plenty of claims, and nine tenths of them crooked! But all that had any sort of proof got their stuff back.

And the rest—about a third of the stuff that we had brought in—was turned over to Lou and to me; and we made it a wedding present. She had her doubts about starting our lives on blood money; but I tried to convince her that she had no right to complain, because if it hadn't been for us, everything would have been lost to the world. And, to make amends for anything that was tainted in that coin, we made our decision to start right in where poor old Daggett had left off.

And that was what we done. It took ten years of hard work. It meant sinking money by the tens of thousands. But across that desert we run a road that nobody would be ashamed to travel on. And the railroad got interested and run up a branch line to the creek. And we cleared the big meadows; and we fed the big trees—or a handy part of them—into the sawmills.

I dunno that this here job has really paid, and I can figure out that if we had put the money out at five per cent in the first place, it would of done a lot more for us in the meantime; but, just the same, we never regret it.

Because, between you and me, we feel that old

117

Daggett himself must know about what's happening, and that it would sure tickle him to see the valley prosper the way it has under us.

The old house is gone. There was too much sorrow in its roots, as you might say. And we put us up a big, rambling careless sort of a log house. But the kids like it, and we like it. And Daggett Creek comes winding and singing and shining right past under our windows. So what more could a body ask?

We hope that you enjoyed reading this
Sagebrush Large Print Western.
If you would like to read more Sagebrush titles,
ask your librarian or contact the Publishers:

United States and Canada

Thomas T. Beeler, *Publisher*
Post Office Box 659
Hampton Falls, New Hampshire 03844-0659
(800) 818-7574

United Kingdom, Eire, and
the Republic of South Africa

Isis Publishing Ltd
7 Centremead
Osney Mead
Oxford OX2 0ES England
(01865) 250333

Australia and New Zealand

Bolinda Publishing Pty. Ltd.
17 Mohr Street
Tullamarine, 3043, Victoria, Australia
(016103) 9338 0666